Mikayla's Victory

Cynthia Bates

James Lorimer & Company Ltd., Publishers
Toronto, 1998

First publication in the United States, 1999

James Lorimer & Company Ltd. acknowledges the support of the Department of Canadian Heritage and the Ontario Arts Council in the development of writing and publishing in Canada. We acknowledge the support of the Canada Council for the Arts for our publishing program.

Cover illustration: Sharif Tarabay

Canadian Cataloguing in Publication Data

Bates, Cynthia, 1950-
    Mikayla's Victory

(Sports stories)
    ISBN 1-55028-639-0 (bound) ISBN 1-55028-638-2 (pbk.)

I. Title. II. Series: Sports stories (Toronto, Ont.).

PS8553.A8263M54 1998   jC813'.54   C98-932336-6
PZ7.B29453Mi 1998

James Lorimer & Company Ltd.,   Distributed in the United States by:
Publishers   Orca Book Publishers
35 Britain Street   P.O. Box 468
Toronto, Ontario   Custer, WA USA
M5A 1R7   98240-0468

Printed and bound in Canada

Contents

To my Mother,
Who always believed in me.

Prologue

Thinking Back ...

Mikayla sat on the grass with her long, muscular legs stretched out in front of her. Her skin, like burnished ebony, glistened with the sweat of her earlier efforts. She gazed out onto the tarmac, steaming in the hot June sun. Soon she would try and set a new record in the senior girls' high jump. The existing record, she knew, had been set fourteen years earlier and was, therefore, the same age as herself. Now she had only to wait until the field judge arrived to measure the bar's height and make sure that everything was official.

She had been jumping well all morning, certainly better than she had ever jumped before. She recalled Coach Bradford's words just minutes earlier: "Mik, you're ready for this. You can do it."

Mikayla also believed she could do it and that alone was a major breakthrough. Although self-confidence had never been her strength, it had certainly improved over the last year, and Mikayla could not help reflecting on the chain of events and challenges that had resulted in that improvement.

Mikayla glanced at her coach. Ms. Bradford looked relaxed, for a change, but Mikayla suspected that her coach was also thinking back to the previous year: same athlete, same event, very different story ...

1

The Challenge

Track and field was the last sport of the year and one of the most popular at Nellie McClung Middle School in Ottawa. Its popularity had as much to do with the fact that making the track team meant two days off school as it did with the love of the sport. Two whole days in the middle of June at the Terry Fox Athletic Facility on the beach of Mooney's Bay, even for those who only made the team in one event. McClung had no shortage of outstanding athletes to secure one more in a long string of championships for the school, but Coaches Bradford and Daniels also encouraged many less talented students to train and participate. It was good for school spirit.

"Ready for the track meeting, Tori?" Mikayla Lamoureux asked her good friend, Victoria Mason, as they returned books to their lockers.

Victoria's response was muttered, "I can't make it, I have another physiotherapy appointment after school."

"Oh, yeah, I forgot." Mikayla paused, then continued with concern. "How's your hamstring doing, anyway?"

"My doctor says a couple more weeks of therapy and absolutely no running or jumping in the meantime. I just hate watching everyone else train!" Victoria pouted, her green eyes flashing. Her skin, usually pale under a light sprinkling of freckles, was flushed with annoyance.

Struck by the momentary change in her friend's appearance, Mikayla reflected on what a contrast her friend's looks were to her own. They both had tall, slender, "athletic bodies," as Coach Bradford would say. Mikayla saw her own body as solid and muscular. Victoria's seemed light and willowy, though Mikayla knew her friend was every bit as strong as she was. And Victoria's skin almost looked translucent next to Mikayla's, which was very dark. Normally, Mikayla went to great efforts to keep her frizzy black hair under control, but she had recently convinced her foster parents to let her get her hair braided in tiny, neat little rows that lay firmly against her head. Though it had taken hours and cost a fortune, she loved the way it looked and felt. It was much easier for sports, too. Victoria, on the other hand, had a full head of long, auburn spirals.

"Why are you staring at me like that?" demanded Victoria. "Did you hear what I said?"

Mikayla brought her attention quickly back to her friend's predicament. "Hey, Tori, cheer up! Two weeks isn't that long," she said sympathetically. "Listen, I'll let Coach Bradford know you're tied up today, but that you'd like to be a team manager until you heal, how's that?" She waved goodbye to her friend and headed toward the gym.

"Thanks, Mik," called Victoria, returning the wave. "I've always wanted to be a star manager."

But Mikayla missed her friend's parting comment. Her thoughts had already turned to a matter of great importance: her quest to become McClung's female entry in the prestigious pentathlon. The pentathlon included five events: the 100- and 800-metre runs, long jump, high jump and shot put. Coach Bradford had mentioned it to her earlier that day in gym class and had asked her to think about it.

"Mik," she'd said, "I have to be honest with you. I'm also considering Amelie Blair. Now, even though you're in grade seven and she's in grade eight, that won't matter in the end because there's no age group for this event. It'll come down to who's best qualified overall and who's willing to work the hardest."

Mikayla had thought of little else all day. She entered the gym and joined a group of friends gathered near the stage. Catching Amelie Blair's eye, Mikayla flashed her a little smile and was surprised when Amelie started walking toward her.

"So," Amelie opened, "it looks like Coach Bradford wants to train the two of us for the pentathlon. You should go for it, Mik. Maybe some of your sprinting speed will rub off on me during practices." She paused a moment, grinning. "Oh, yeah, and I'll borrow a few centimetres off your long jump, too!"

Mikayla was tongue-tied for a moment. It seemed that everyone at McClung knew Amelie, who was the president of the girls' athletic association. But, although she had played with Amelie on house league teams, Mikayla didn't know her well enough to tell whether this teasing was good-natured or spiteful. "Well," she finally stammered, "I … I'll do my best to push you so I, I mean, so you … "

"You do that," Amelie interrupted, flashing a conspiratorial wink before sauntering away, leaving Mikayla completely bewildered. Amelie seems so sure of herself compared to me, Mikayla thought. I probably don't have a chance against her.

Amelie was the most popular girl at McClung. From what Mikayla knew about her, Amelie's popularity was the result of her friendly, outgoing and — according to some — outrageous personality. Now Mikayla wondered if the pentathlon competition might reveal another side of Amelie that she hadn't seen before.

The information meeting was brief; the coaches made their usual pitch for everyone to work hard and promised that, if they did, a place would be made for them on the team.

Those unable to compete would be managers. That reminded Mikayla of Victoria and she made her way over to where the coaches were collecting names of interested students according to age and gender.

"Sorry, Mik," Coach Bradford smiled, "I've got bantam boys here and, if I'm not mistaken, you're an intermediate girl."

"Very funny, Coach." Mikayla returned the smile. "Actually, I just wanted to let you know that Tori is at a physio appointment this afternoon, but she really wants to help out with track. Is there something she could do?"

"So that hamstring is still being treated, is it?" Ms. Bradford frowned. "Well, no problem giving her some work to do. I can always use a little organizational assistance."

"Great, I'll let her know," replied Mikayla.

"See you tomorrow after school for the first high jump practice. Tell Victoria to come along too and I'll get her started on record-keeping."

Mikayla gave her name to Mr. Daniels, the boys' gym teacher, and sprinted over to where her friends were filing out of the gym, talking excitedly about their events and how well they hoped to do. She had told no one but Tori about trying out for the pentathlon but, knowing how the grapevine worked, she was pretty sure that it would already be old news by lunchtime tomorrow. Her head was so full of track and tryouts and her peculiar exchange with Amelia Blair, she almost forgot about her mother's upcoming visit. Almost.

2

Friends and Family

Mikayla walked home from school with David Cook, as she had done almost every day throughout the year. Gradually, he had become the only friend she trusted enough to share her confused feelings about her family. All of Mikayla's other friends seemed to lead such "normal" lives. As close as she had become to Victoria since they'd arrived at McClung in September, from different schools, Tori's life still just seemed too storybook perfect for Mikayla to feel comfortable talking about the complexities of her own family life. David wasn't in quite the same crazy situation as Mikayla, not by a long shot. But his father was black, his mother was white and, while David usually felt good about being both, he had confided to Mikayla that at times he felt like he was neither.

"How's life at the Carrigan house?" David asked with a smile.

It was a smile that opened Mikayla's heart every time she saw it, and she forced herself to look away from her friend's face so she could consider her response. Besides being a good listener, David was, in Mikayla's opinion, the best-looking guy at McClung. His skin was quite a bit fairer than hers and he wore his dark, curly hair short. He had gentle, brown eyes and perfect teeth which Mikayla envied. It didn't seem quite fair that David's father was an orthodontist, seeing as David would probably never need braces, while Mikayla was going to have to get them this summer.

"Well? Are you going to answer me, dreamer?" David asked playfully.

"I was thinking!" Mikayla replied, trying to cover her lapse in attention. "Things are pretty good, I guess. I mean, Jan and Taylor are great! But I still worry that it's not going to last."

"What do you mean?"

"It's hard to explain," she responded slowly. "I guess it's not always that easy to just be myself. What if they decide they don't like me after all if I let my bad moods show or ... or if I lose my temper sometimes?"

David took Mikayla by the elbow and turned her to face him. "Mik," he said gently, "that's not going to happen. The Carrigans are good people." When Mikayla didn't respond, he added, "Hey! Did I ever tell you that Jason used to babysit me?"

Mikayla laughed, "Only about a million times. He taught you everything you know about basketball, right?"

David smiled, then continued, serious again. "Jan and Taylor, and Jason, too, care a lot about you. You know, it's been almost two years that you've been with them. It's time to start trusting them."

Mikayla responded cautiously, "Well ... it *seems* like they're proud of me and they don't seem to mind having me around."

"Trust me, Mik, you've got nothing to worry about."

They continued walking and let the subject drift to school, sports and mutual friends. Before she knew it, David was turning down his own street several blocks before hers.

Now Mikayla couldn't help thinking about her mother, who would be visiting the following day for the first time in awhile. She remembered how stressful the last visit had been, just before her mother's most recent heart attack. Nothing had changed. Mikayla and Angeline, her seven-year-old sister, were still in foster care, and Mikayla's mother was still chronically ill with little hope of ever being well enough to care for her daughters.

Mikayla pictured her mother, Noelle. Several old, ragged photographs she had tucked away showed Mikayla as a young child standing beside her. The pictures had been taken before the two left Mikayla's birthplace in the Caribbean. Mikayla thought that her mother had been beautiful then, but now, only eight years later, Noelle bore little resemblance to that smiling, youthful face in the pictures. At the age of 28, her mother lived in a nursing home because of her poor health. She was terribly thin and her complexion had paled to a sickly shade of grey.

Mikayla could hardly remember a time when her mother had been strong and healthy. Her earliest memories were of Noelle napping on the couch, completely exhausted. The reason for her mother's constant fatigue had been discovered when, days after arriving in Ottawa, Noelle had visited a neighbourhood clinic, complaining of exhaustion and shortness of breath. The clinic had sent her for tests which revealed a congenital, degenerative heart condition. The situation was further complicated by the discovery that Noelle was pregnant with her second child.

Although Mikayla didn't know all the details, she had heard enough whispered conversations between her mother and her Great-Auntie Hallie, with whom they were living at the time, to know that her mother had fled to Canada in order to escape a disastrous marriage. Asking Mikayla's father for help seemed to have been out of the question. They were on their own, with only Noelle's old auntie to help them.

It hadn't gone well. Noelle had nearly died during the birth of Mikayla's sister, Angeline. She had been required to

remain in hospital for several weeks afterward and Angeline
had been put into foster care. Within months of Noelle coming home from the hospital, Great-Auntie Hallie had passed
away, leaving Mikayla and her mother to fend for themselves.

Mikayla knew her mother had tried hard but, in her weak-
ened state, Noelle needed to spend most of her time resting.
Mikayla gradually learned how to look after herself and to
tend to her mother's needs. But she was only a six-year-old
girl and, although Noelle's health improved a little, Mikayla
took most of the responsibility for tidying the apartment and
getting meals. Mikayla remembered the day her mother, in
tears, had told her that she, too, would have to go into foster
care.

Mikayla sighed. That was over six years ago and Mikayla
had not lived with her mother since. Noelle had suffered two
heart attacks in that time and the combination of her fragile
health and the effects of some of her medications had caused
her to become irritable and easily confused. Mikayla's rela-
tionship with her mother had grown increasingly strained as
the young girl struggled to fit into foster homes. Now Mikayla
found herself apprehensive before every visit.

At least I'll get to see Angeline, she thought, and that gave
her some comfort. Angeline lived in another foster home
outside of Ottawa. The Lincolns were a wealthy black couple
who owned a construction company. They had been unable to
have children of their own and had taken Angeline in as an
infant. Mikayla liked the Lincolns and knew that they loved
Angeline dearly, but they lived so far away that Mikayla saw
her sister only occasionally. Thinking of Angeline and how
much she missed her only increased Mikayla's anxiety.

Lost in thought, Mikayla's feet led her straight to the front
porch where her foster mother, Janice Carrigan, was coming
down the steps toward her with a big smile.

"Hi, Mik! How was your day?" Without waiting for a response, she continued, "I'm just running up to Bank Street for some fruit. Want to come along?"

"Thanks, Jan, but I've got a ton of homework I'd better get started on."

"Okay. Taylor just got home. I'll be back shortly."

Mikayla entered the house where she lived with Jan and Taylor Carrigan, the middle-aged couple who had welcomed her as a foster child only two years previously, after her stays in three other homes had fallen through. Mikayla knew those failures had not been her fault, they had only been intended as temporary placements in the first place. But that had not kept her from hoping each time that things might become permanent.

After so much disappointment, Mikayla had almost given up hope of fitting in anywhere. But the Carrigans had been a surprise — a white couple with an older son of their own who lived at home and attended the local university. Jason was a member of his school's basketball team and he occasionally took time out from his studies and team responsibilities to work with Mikayla and her friends on their basketball skills. He was patient and encouraging, and Mikayla had a lot of respect for him.

As for Jan and Taylor, Mikayla was very fond of them. They were understanding but firm, open-minded, flexible and affectionate, but reserved. Jan worked part-time at home writing computer programs and Taylor was a high school English teacher.

Only one aspect of her placement with the Carrigans made Mikayla uncomfortable. That was the fact that it was not easy being black in her foster family's white world. Certainly, the Carrigans never said or did anything to create Mikayla's sense of discomfort. She could not explain it; it was just there.

"Is that you, Mikayla?" Taylor Carrigan called from the back of the house. "Come here for a minute. I've got something to show you."

Mikayla made her way to the family room and sat down on the couch across from Taylor. She smiled at her foster father and momentarily considered her good fortune to have been placed with such a generous, warm-hearted family. Her family, that's how she thought of them. At school, she sometimes referred to Jan and Taylor as her "mom and dad." Her closest friends knew Mikayla's situation and tried to be sensitive to her feelings, but Mikayla was a very private person and her life was a source of some mystery, even to those who knew her best.

Taylor handed her a section of the newspaper with an article circled in red. Mikayla read with increasing excitement; the local track club was planning to run a day camp for youth throughout the summer that would train them in all track and field events. To Mikayla, it sounded like the perfect way to spend part of the long summer break.

"What do you think, Taylor? Can I sign up?" She didn't want to get her hopes up, in case they couldn't afford it.

"Well, we'll talk it over with Jan at supper," Taylor responded mildly. "Don't forget, you're already registered for the university basketball camp."

"I know, and I can't wait, but that's only one week. This camp sounds so awesome. I could contribute my babysitting savings toward it."

Taylor smiled at that. Mikayla was often teased good-naturedly by family members about how "careful" (Jason used the word "tight") she was with her hard-earned money. She was fairly sure her offer to pay part of the expense would seal it.

"We'll see, Mikayla."

It was always "we'll see," but Mikayla was optimistic as she made her way upstairs to her room.

3

Victoria's Miraculous Cure

Victoria and Mikayla met at their lockers before school the following morning. Mikayla's face shone with a thin layer of perspiration. She had already been out for a training run.

"Man," enthused Mikayla, "Coach Bradford is one demanding running coach!"

"How far did she have you run this morning?" asked Victoria.

"I just did three slow laps of the park, a little over a kilometre. Some of the others had trouble finishing two laps! I think Coach B. is going to have to ease up a little if she wants to keep everyone interested in training. But, hey, you should have seen Max, Tori. He ran four laps easily, and probably could have gone around a few more times, but I think he wanted to get back to school to see a certain red-headed track manager."

"Cut it out, Mik. 'Track manager' sounds so ... I don't know, so nerdy!" Victoria grinned. "Speaking of Max, he called last night! Said he had some big surprise for me today, something to do with my hamstring. By the way, not to change the subject, but are your mom and Angeline still coming today?"

As Mikayla started to answer Victoria's question, the first bell interrupted, as did the appearance of Maxwell St. John, coming up behind an unsuspecting Victoria.

Victoria jumped as Max gave her a gentle poke in the back. "Jeepers, Max, you scared me!"

Max, his blond hair tousled and still wet from the shower, replied, "Victoria Mason, I've got a wicked surprise for you. Just a minute."

Max shifted down to his own locker and quickly unlocked and opened it. He pulled out a large, clear plastic bag containing what appeared to be an enormous rectangular bandage. One side was very dark brown in colour and, when Max flipped it over to the other side, Mikayla noticed that the label was written in Chinese characters. Max, with a big grin on his impish face, looked very pleased with himself.

"What the heck ..." But Victoria's question was cut short as Max opened the bag and the three friends were overcome by the pungent odour of its contents. Other students passing in the hall reacted similarly, waving the air in front of their faces and grimacing as the unusual odour reached them. The smell, Mikayla thought, was actually not unpleasant, simply overpoweringly strong. Max sealed the bag back up quickly.

"We're going to be late. I'll explain in homeroom." He grabbed some books from his locker and they headed upstairs to their classroom.

* * *

After morning classes ended, Mikayla waited at her locker for Victoria, who was writing a geography make-up test. Across the hall, she saw Amelie Blair pause at the door of the lunchroom and peer inside. Several of Amelie's friends were seated together at one of the back tables but apparently they were not the objects of her search. Amelie turned away from the crowded room and caught up with Raymond Ling in the hall headed toward the exit to the schoolyard.

Mikayla continued putting away her books from morning classes when she saw Ms. Bradford step out of her office and walk casually down the corridor in the direction Amelie and Raymond had gone. Mikayla wondered momentarily why the coach seemed to be following them, but she suddenly remembered that she had something to tell Ms. Bradford herself.

"Coach!" Mikayla called, approaching her teacher from behind.

"Hi, Mik. What's up?"

"Guess what? The most incredible thing has happened with Tori's injury!"

"Well, Mikayla," the coach responded with a smile, "don't keep me in suspense. What is it?"

"Okay, Max was at Van Canh Le's house yesterday after school and he and V.C. were talking about how it's too bad Tori won't be able to run track because of her leg. Before he knows it, V.C.'s mother is rummaging around in their kitchen cupboards and she comes out with this big, stinky, sticky patch. She tells them it's a good Chinese remedy for sore muscles."

"Uh huh?" Coach Bradford continued for Mikayla. "So Max brings it to Victoria for her hamstring, and ... ?"

"And she's had it on all morning. Now nobody will go within ten metres of her — except me, and Max, of course."

"Of course."

Mikayla took a breath. "But the most incredible thing is, her leg doesn't hurt anymore! Honestly, you won't believe this. She's walking completely normally!"

"Mikayla, that *is* wonderful news!" the coach responded. "You be sure and tell Victoria to see me after school at the high jump practice. You'll be there too?"

"Yes ..." Mikayla answered hesitantly, "but I'm really nervous about high jump. The only time I ever tried it was in gym class the other day."

"And you showed excellent potential, Mikayla. It's not the easiest skill and it requires lots of practice, so we'll see you after school," Coach Bradford concluded as she glanced toward the exit then turned back in the direction of her office.

Great, thought Mikayla. First a practice with Amelie Blair, last year's high jump gold medalist, then a little visit with Mom. What else could happen to make my day?

4

The First Practice

Seventeen girls showed up for the high jump practice. Victoria Mason was one of them — and she showed up dressed to participate. Mikayla watched as Coach Bradford took Victoria gently by the arm and nodded to Pauline to start the warm-up. Pauline Duvall was a university student who had done volunteer work in the McClung gym program for the past two years. This year Coach Bradford had given her the responsibility of coaching high jump. Mikayla remembered her first gym class in the fall when Ms. Bradford had introduced Pauline.

"Girls, I would like you to meet someone special," Ms. Bradford had said, indicating a short, but very fit-looking, young, black woman standing next to her. "This is Pauline Duvall." The young woman smiled broadly at the class.

"Pauline is working on a Masters' degree in physical education at Ottawa U. Last year she started volunteering by coming in every Tuesday and Thursday to assist me with gym classes and coaching. We are very lucky to have her back again this year." Ms. Bradford smiled fondly at Pauline and continued. "What makes Pauline special to me is the fact that she was a student of mine here at McClung several years ago."

Ms. Bradford waited for murmured responses from the seated students to die down before going on. "Some of you may have noticed that Pauline's is one of the names on the Top Athlete trophy in the display case."

"That's why her name seems so familiar," Mikayla whispered to Victoria.

"Pauline, would you mind telling the girls a little about yourself?" Ms. Bradford requested.

The young woman spoke in a strong voice, making eye contact with the group. "Well, I grew up here in Ottawa. My parents immigrated from Haiti just before I was born. When I came to McClung, I hadn't played a lot of sports. I was pretty scrawny."

The girls laughed.

"Anyway," she continued, smiling, "Ms. Bradford got me participating in everything in the gym and I loved it. She even made me try high jump, which is a pretty unusual event for someone my size, but I was lucky enough to win a medal at it in grade eight."

Again, there was some reaction from the girls. "Cool!" and "All *right!*" could be heard from some of the more enthusiastic class members.

"Mainly though," Pauline carried on, "I got into basketball. And you might think, 'she's too short for basketball.' Fortunately, Coach Bradford didn't seem to think so."

"Hardly," Ms. Bradford interjected. "We won the city championship with Pauline at point guard."

"Yeah, I'll never forget that," Pauline responded. "Then I went to high school and kept playing. In my final year, our team made it to O.F.S.S.A.A., that's the provincial high school championships, and we won bronze medals. I was recruited by York University to play on their women's team and that was where I was for five years before coming back to Ottawa." She grinned. "End of story."

Mikayla led her gym class in a spontaneous burst of applause.

"Thanks," Pauline said, "but what I really want you to get out of all this is the knowledge that you can do anything if you believe in yourself and are willing to work hard. Doesn't matter if you're short, tall, skinny, fat, white, black or green."

Mikayla remembered the expressions on the faces of her classmates. Most of them had been as impressed as she was. From that moment on, Pauline had become her role model.

"What do you mean, should you go for it?" Pauline demanded when Mikayla had asked her advice about competing with Amelie for the pentathlon. "Can you come up with one good reason why you shouldn't?"

And Mikayla couldn't, so here she was, scared silly of making a fool of herself, but more frightened of not trying at all.

Amelie Blair appeared in the gym just as the warm-up was ending. Mikayla watched Pauline note Amelie's lateness on her clipboard, then tell her to jog a few laps and do some stretching on her own.

Mikayla saw the disappointment on Victoria's face as soon as she re-entered the gym. She motioned for her friend to join her.

"What happened? Do you get to practise?" Mikayla asked in a low voice.

"Nope," Victoria paused. "Coach says she believes in herbal remedies and 'the healing powers of non-traditional medicine.'" Victoria mimicked the voice and gestures of her coach and Mikayla could hear the edge of her friend's disappointment.

"But?"

"She says that I have to get a letter from the doctor giving me permission to train," explained Victoria. "Fat chance! My doctor said at least two weeks off with physio, and not a day less!"

Mikayla put a comforting hand on her friend's shoulder but she was at a loss for words. Pauline was signalling Victoria to come over and help her run the practice so, with a shrug at Mikayla, Victoria made her way over to where Pauline was organizing the jumpers.

About half of the girls at the practice were grade sevens and therefore had little training in high jump. The basics had been introduced in gym class and Coach Bradford had recruited a few promising girls to come out to the practice. The rest of the girls were grade eights who had made the team the previous year as jumpers or alternates.

"I wonder if Coach B. is going to pick Ammi for the pentathlon," Mikayla overheard Quyen Ha say to another one of Amelie's friends while they waited their turn to jump the warm-up height.

"Who else would she choose? Ammi's got it made. She told me herself she didn't think she had any serious competition," responded the other girl.

The girls were close friends of Amelie's, so Mikayla wasn't surprised at their assumption. Nevertheless, it hurt her feelings to know that Amelie did not consider her a serious contender.

"Quyen, it's your jump," Pauline called.

Quyen, with her straight, shoulder-length jet black hair flying behind her, approached the crossbar and sailed over easily, snapping her legs perfectly and landing like a feather in the crash pad. Mikayla guessed that she had lost none of her form from the previous year when she had taken the silver medal to Amelie's gold.

While Quyen was certainly an accomplished jumper, Mikayla suspected that she was not seriously interested in track and field. She knew that it was the only sport Quyen had gone out for all year. It seemed that her social life was the priority this year. And Mikayla had no doubt that Quyen had a full social life. She carried herself with an air of quiet but confident sophistication, almost mysterious. She was flawlessly beautiful, smart enough to be in the gifted class, and multi-talented. Nevertheless, she was probably out for track just to keep Amelie company and to get two days off school in order to soak up the June sun and meet boys from other schools.

It was Amelie's turn to jump. She began by flashing a huge grin. Next, she strolled casually up to the crossbar as if pacing off her approach. She stood still for a moment at the waist-high bar. Suddenly, to the delight of everyone present except Pauline, who appeared unamused, Amelie performed a standing scissors jump over the bar, landing on her feet in the pit, having cleared the bar by several centimetres.

"Ammi, you're supposed to be practising your approach and proper technique," Pauline addressed her firmly. "Let's see a more serious effort on your next attempt."

Surprisingly unconcerned, Amelie grinned again. "No problem, Pauline. I'll be good next time."

Mikayla regarded Amelie as she skipped back to where her friends awaited her, clearly delighted with her antics. Even Pauline, shaking her head, was trying to hide a smile. Amelie struck Mikayla as someone with whom it would be difficult to stay annoyed. She had a friendly, open face that was usually smiling, and a mop of brown curls that allowed her to play the clown when she felt like it, which was often. When it came to being an athlete, though, Amelie could adopt the serious concentration of a champion. And it was well-known that she had the talent of a champion in several different sports.

The rest of the practice was uneventful. Despite being extremely nervous, especially in Amelie's presence, Mikayla was easily able to jump the low heights Pauline had set.

Amelie not only settled down, she became increasingly subdued as the practice continued.

Mikayla left early to go home and prepare for the visit of
her mother and sister. She had just walked in the door when
the phone rang.

It was Victoria, sounding agitated and flustered.

"Mik, I'm calling from school," Victoria began breath-
lessly. "You will not believe what happened at the end of
practice!"

"Well?" Mikayla responded.

"It's Amelie. I think she's got a problem," Victoria continued, in a low whisper.

Mikayla became immediately attentive as Victoria relayed
what occurred after Mikayla had left.

"Amelie was sick," Victoria began. "She ran out of the
gym right after her last jump. I followed her to the locker
room and found her down on her knees with her head in the
toilet, throwing up."

"Yecch!" responded Mikayla. "I don't get it, she seemed
all right when I left."

Victoria continued, "Yeah, well, anyway, I asked her if she
was okay, but she kept groaning and retching and couldn't
really answer, so I just stayed there with her. She finally
stopped throwing up, but she was still moaning when Pauline
showed up."

"What did *she* do?" Mikayla inquired, now very interested.

"She said she'd look after her," Victoria responded. "So I
backed off and waited a few minutes. Amelie finally got up.
She looked really pale and a little nervous. She thanked me
for helping and said she'd be fine. I just changed and got the
heck out of there!"

Mikayla was puzzled. "Nervous? Why do you say she
looked nervous?"

"Mik," Victoria answered, "I couldn't say for sure, but, when Amelie was throwing up, it sure smelled like alcohol."

"You're kidding!" exclaimed Mikayla. "You think she'd been drinking?"

"I'm not positive, but it was like when my sister came home after her grad party and she was so sick. The smell was the same. And Pauline had the same look on her face today that my parents had with my sister!"

"So what happened? Where's Amelie now?" Mikayla asked.

"Pauline just walked her out to the yard. Her dad usually picks her up after practices."

"Wow," responded Mikayla. "I wonder what's going on."

"Me too," agreed Victoria. "It's just that, well, I know you and Ammi are competing against each other right now, and you know I want you to get the pentathlon, but ..." she trailed off.

"But what?" Mikayla urged.

"Well, Ammi has always been so friendly ... I really hate to think of her being in any kind of serious trouble," Victoria admitted. "Let's not say anything until we know what's going on. I could be wrong."

"Well ..." Mikayla thought it over. "I guess that's okay for now. Her getting into trouble isn't exactly the way I want to win that pentathlon!"

"Yeah, everything's got to be 'fair and square' with you, doesn't it, Mik?" Victoria teased.

"Oh, cut it out, Tori, I'd just rather get the pentathlon because Coach B. thinks I can do the job, that's all," Mikayla responded good-naturedly. "See you tomorrow."

"Bye."

5

Meeting with Mama

Mikayla squirmed in her chair. She wished that they had remained at the Carrigan home rather than going out to a neighbourhood restaurant. She had already seen two kids she knew from school walking by on their way home and one of the families she regularly babysat for was sitting on the other side of the dining room. She knew she shouldn't be embarrassed, but Mikayla couldn't help thinking that theirs was a pretty bizarre-looking party. She was relieved that the meal was over.

"Mikayla, are you listening to me?"

Mikayla cringed. Her mother's voice seemed so loud. "Yes, of course I'm listening, Mama. You were telling me that Angeline got all *A*s and *B*s on her last report card." Mikayla turned to her younger sister, seated beside her. "I'm so proud of you, Angie. You must work really hard."

The little girl's eyes grew moist. "Oh, Mikki, I sure wish I could see you more. No one listens to me like you, so I just stay in my room and read. *That's* why I do so good in school."

Sarah Duncan, the girls' case worker, spoke up. "Why, Angie, I thought you were happy at the Lincolns'. You *do* like them, don't you?"

"Of course she likes them. She's got a good life with that family," interjected Noelle Lamoureux irritably.

"Mama, let Angie talk," pleaded Mikayla. She knew her mother's heart condition made her tired and a little grouchy at times but she also recognized how hard it was for her little sister to understand that.

"Mrs. Lamoureux," Jan Carrigan said, laying a gentle hand on the agitated woman's arm. "Why don't we walk back to our house? The fresh air will do us all good."

Mikayla's mother eyed Jan suspiciously for a moment, then appeared to relax and reached for her purse. She started to get up, "I guess I'm just worn out."

Mikayla rose hastily and went to her mother's side, taking her gently by the arm. "Mama," she said, "maybe you should let Ms. Duncan take you home. You look awfully tired."

Noelle patted her daughter's arm, "I'll be all right, Mikki. Come on, walk with your mama and tell me all about your running and jumping. It sounds to me like you're headed for the Olympics!"

"Oh, Mama," Mikayla laughed, "don't tease me!" But Mikayla was encouraged by her mother's sudden lightheartedness. A glance at Angeline, tagging along happily beside her, convinced Mikayla that the previous moment's tension had been broken.

But Noelle was in a nostalgic mood.

"You know I did my best for you, don't you, Mikki?" she was asking. "I wasn't much more than a girl myself when my mama sent you and me up here."

"Why to Canada?" Jan asked softly, turning back toward Noelle and her daughters.

"I had an old auntie living in Ottawa," Noelle answered. "My mama thought we could have a good life here, and maybe I could get better medical attention."

"And did you?" Jan urged.

"Well, at least I found out what was wrong with me," Noelle responded quietly. "Not much could be done about it, though."

"I guess things got pretty bad after you had Angeline."

Mikayla could hear the sympathy in Jan's voice as she encouraged Noelle to share her story.

"Sure did," Noelle responded, her voice softening to barely a whisper. "I was real sick. Couldn't look after my baby. She had to go into that foster home. The Lincolns'."

Mikayla knew the story. Her mother had almost reached the part that Mikayla could begin to remember herself when they finally reached the Carrigan home. Everyone was led to the family room and made comfortable while Taylor went to the kitchen to prepare coffee. When the discussion resumed, Mikayla asked her social worker why Angeline had to remain in a foster home where she seemed so miserable.

Sarah Duncan responded, "Mikayla, I know how hard it must be for you to feel that your sister is unhappy. But we know the Lincolns to be an excellent foster family. Angeline has lived there practically since she was born and they love her as if she were their own." She paused and drew a deep breath. "In fact, they have asked your mother for permission to adopt Angeline. I imagine this results in very confusing feelings for your sister."

Mikayla's jaw dropped. She glanced at Angeline, who was staring at the floor.

Ms. Duncan continued, "I know it's a shock, but the Lincolns have had this in mind for some time. In fact, they had wanted to adopt Angie from the beginning, but they had always thought that Noelle might eventually regain custody."

"I sure would have liked to!" Noelle interjected forcefully. "But it was impossible — I was too tired to get out of bed. You remember, Mikki? After Hallie passed on, you ended up doing all the work around the house." She reflected for a moment. "And you were just a little thing yourself."

Mikayla found herself weeping. "Mama," she whispered, "what about Angie?"

"Mrs. Lamoureux," Sarah Duncan took over for the emotionally distressed girl, "we know you love Mikayla and Angeline, and *they* know that it's because of that love that you allowed them to go into foster care. But if they adopt her, the Lincolns can provide many opportunities for Angeline that are not available in a foster care situation."

Noelle turned away from the young social worker and looked at her eldest daughter. Mikayla felt like her mother was trying to look into her heart for the right thing to do.

Finally she stood up. "Ms. Duncan," she said calmly, "I think I'd like to go now."

She walked over to Angeline and gathered her youngest daughter into her arms. "Little Angel," she began, "that's just what you looked like when you were born, a little angel."

"Yes, Mama," whispered Angeline.

"Mrs. Lamoureux," Sarah Duncan persisted gently, "what about the adoption papers? Will you sign them?"

Noelle ignored the worker and continued talking to Angeline. "Honey, you don't have to be afraid of being happy on my account."

Angeline looked stricken. It was obvious that she did not want her mother to hurt.

"It's not that I don't love you, baby," Noelle continued, her voice sounding hollow. Her attention appeared to be drifting as she finished quietly, "The Lord knows I always loved my girls."

It was a heavy, painful moment that seemed suspended, motionless, in the room. Like something out of a soap opera, thought Mikayla, only this is real, this is my life.

She was relieved when Ms. Duncan rose from her chair and gathered her purse and briefcase to leave. She guessed that the social worker would succeed now in getting her mother to sign Angeline's adoption papers. But she wasn't sure how her sister would accept such a decision. Despite having lived most of her life with her foster family, Angeline had a deep love for and loyalty to her mother. Mikayla recognized that her sister's adoption would just be a formality, but she couldn't quite shake the fear that Angeline's gaining a family meant that Mikayla would lose a sister.

"I'll be back in about an hour to pick up Angeline," Ms. Duncan said to Jan and Taylor. "She and Mikki can have a nice little visit, just the two of them."

At the last minute, Mikayla rushed to the front door, threw her arms around her mother's neck and whispered fiercely in her ear, "I love you, Mama. I really love you." Before Noelle could respond, Mikayla was rushing down the hallway to the family room, and back to one of the only people in the world she knew loved her unconditionally, her little Angeline.

6

The Killer Run

Apparently recovered from her mysterious illness, Amelie showed up for middle distance practice the following morning where she and Mikayla, along with other track hopefuls, were expected to run their first time trial for the 800-metre race. It was a glorious morning. The sun was warm and a gentle breeze would keep the runners from overheating.

Mikayla loved running in Heritage Park, which acted as both a track and a playing field for her school. Her coaches had commented frequently on how lucky the school was to have the use of this greenspace, which was located just a five-minute walk from the school, under the highway overpass, and at the edge of an old, affluent neighbourhood.

Nellie McClung Middle School was located in Ottawa's Centretown and was surrounded by asphalt, concrete, closely-set older residences, apartment and office buildings, restaurants, a bowling alley and a car wash. On the east side of the block was Bank Street, one of the city's busiest and most interesting roadways. Across the street from the school to the west was the sprawling Voyageur Bus Terminal, and to the south ran the Queensway, a busy eight-lane expressway that linked Ottawa with Toronto and Montreal.

Heritage Park filled an area equaling two large city blocks. The trees were massive, the grass well-tended, and huge bushes rimmed the perimeter. Flower beds were planted here and there and park benches were scattered along the fine gravel paths that wound throughout the park and on which McClung students ran.

"Listen up, girls and guys," Coach Bradford was saying. "Please stretch while I give you some instructions." She waited until everyone had begun warming-up. "This is just a preliminary time trial. You are not competing with each other," she continued with emphasis. "Just try and run your own personal best. Today's results will not determine who makes or doesn't make the team."

Mr. Daniels continued with the instructions. "The path around the park is approximately 600 metres long, so your total run is one and one-third laps of the park. You start where we're standing, run one full lap and, on the second lap, you finish at the third lamp post up the path on the left." He pointed to where the coaches would be standing at the finish line. "Now this is important. Ms. Bradford and I will be calling out your times as you finish your run. You'll be very tired, but you must listen so you can report your time to Victoria."

"Okay, is everyone ready?" asked Coach Bradford. "The intermediate and senior boys will start first. One minute later, the bantam boys and senior girls will start. Mikayla, I want you to run with that group today."

There were seven or eight runners in each group. Max St. John and Van Canh Le were only intermediates but they, along with one of the big senior runners, led the first group. Max was the school's top male runner in middle and long distance events. Van Canh was primarily a sprinter, a school record holder in the 100 and 200, but he could run with the best at almost any distance under 1500 metres.

Amelie and Mikayla went out in the second group and quickly left the smaller bantam boys and two other girls behind. Like Van Canh, Mikayla was built for speed and was unbeatable in the shorter distances. Eight hundred metres, however, was a new experience for her. She instinctively started fast. Partway around the first lap of the park she glanced over her shoulder and saw Amelie five metres back, looking comfortable. When Mikayla passed the halfway mark in the run, Amelie was still several metres behind.

Suddenly, Mikayla's lungs felt like they were on fire and her legs started to feel heavy. To her dismay and despite all efforts to prevent it, her body started to slow down. Each stride became increasingly painful. She was gulping in air. As Mikayla completed the first lap, Amelie sailed by, picking up speed as she headed into the final stretch.

Hurting, Mikayla continued losing speed. She was aware of a leaden sensation in her legs as two bantam boys ran by her, twenty metres before the finish. Discouraged, Mikayla carried on in slow motion, her lungs burning, while an intermediate girl, who had started a minute after her, also went by.

Ms. Bradford grabbed Mikayla as she stumbled, exhausted and gasping for air, across the finish line. The coach forced her to continue walking, taking deep breaths until she began to cool down.

"Mik," Ms. Bradford soothed, "it's like that for everyone the first time they run the 800. You've got to learn how to run it properly, so be patient, okay? Next time you ..."

"Next time?" gasped Mikayla. "There isn't going to be a next time. I will *never* put myself through that again!"

The coach laughed. "You say that now but, trust me, once you've recovered, you'll want, more than anything, to try it again! I'm sure you don't want to hear this now, but all you have to do is take that incredible 400-metre speed of yours and spread it out. Think about having to run the 400 twice. How would you do it?"

By now, they had stopped walking. Physically, Mikayla was starting to recover and she was already considering her coach's advice. They started back to the finish area.

"Sorry, Tori," said Mikayla to her friend, "I'm afraid I wasn't listening for my time at the finish."

"Don't worry, Mik, I got it," responded Victoria, "but are you okay? I was afraid you were going to collapse!"

Mikayla smiled weakly, "Yeah, I'll live. So what was my time?"

Victoria winced, "Mik, the good news is that you ran the first 400 in 1:05."

"And the 800?" Mikayla persisted.

"3:27."

Mikayla frowned. "How about Amelie? Her time must have been pretty good."

"Only because you set such a brutal pace, Mik!" comforted Victoria. "Ammi had to try and stay close to you because she had no way of knowing if you could keep going at that speed."

"Her time?" Mikayla repeated.

"Ammi ran a 2:43. She says it's the best time she's ever run!" answered Victoria.

Mikayla soon began to feel better as friends gathered around to compare their experiences with the run. Heading to the school, they teased Mikayla good-naturedly and offered her their "professional" advice on her next attempt. David was waiting for her in the schoolyard and she asked him how his high jump practice had gone, hoping to avoid any further discussion of her fiasco with the 800.

"It was great!" he replied. "Pauline taught us how to count out the number of steps to use for our approach and mark a starting spot. Then we mainly worked on jump technique."

Mikayla could see that David was really excited about jumping and she responded just often enough to keep him talking all the way to their lockers.

"Hey, Mik, let's see if anyone wants to go to the movie that starts this weekend at Capital Place," David suggested enthusiastically.

"Sounds good!" Mikayla responded. As long as it doesn't interfere with my new training schedule, she thought. Coach B. was right, I *do* want to improve that 800 performance and, with enough practice, just maybe I will!

7

What's Up with Amelie?

Mikayla was preoccupied throughout her morning classes. When she wasn't thinking about the previous evening with her mother and sister, she was reliving the humiliation of the morning's run. Lunch arrived at last and, with no scheduled practices for her events, Mikayla rushed to the locker room and changed into her running clothes. She jogged lightly to Heritage Park, stretched briefly, then began to run, alternating fast quarter laps of the park with slow easy ones.

Despite having just completed a difficult run a few hours earlier, Mikayla felt strong and energized and was easily able to complete two and a half laps. Unfortunately, she had neglected to use the washroom before leaving school and was suddenly aware of a pressing need.

I'll just slip into the bushes, like up at the cottage, Mikayla thought with amusement. However, any urgency she felt vanished as she peered out from her sheltered hiding place to see Amelie, Raymond, Quyen and another girl entering the park. She was certain they hadn't seen her and, too embarrassed to step out and casually admit to the extra training and the "pit stop," Mikayla decided she would just have to wait until they left.

Mikayla noted with interest that Amelie seemed to be paired up with Raymond Ling again. Raymond didn't seem to Mikayla like a "bad" kid exactly, but he had repeated grade eight at McClung and was therefore older than his classmates. The friends he hung out with were grade nines at Elgin Collegiate and, rumour had it, they were in a fair amount of trouble at school: cutting classes, failing courses and intimidating other students. They were definitely known in the community where Mikayla lived, and there had been rumours of drug use.

The group gathered around a picnic table about thirty metres from Mikayla. She could see them clearly, but she could not make out what they were saying. She saw one girl take cigarettes out of her bag and offer them around. Everyone took one. Mikayla was not surprised at the rest of them, but she was shocked to see Amelie light the cigarette expertly, inhale deeply and blow the smoke out of her mouth with the ease of a seasoned smoker. While it seemed that smoking had become a "cool" thing to do among certain McClung students, Mikayla wondered what would possess Amelie to jeopardize her health and her athletic talents to take up such a disgusting habit!

It got worse. A few minutes later, two of Raymond's high school buddies showed up, obviously expected by the younger group. Quyen and the girl Mikayla hadn't recognized each approached one of the new arrivals with cheerful greetings and hugs. One of the older boys withdrew two bottles from his bag and placed them on the picnic table. The bottles — Mikayla could not tell whether they were wine or liquor but knew that they weren't soft drinks — were passed around and shared by everyone.

Mikayla felt sick. Although she was competing with her for the pentathlon position, she had to admit that Amelie had been an incredible example to the school's female athletes all year. Mikayla knew that Victoria, who had known Amelie for a couple of years and greatly admired her, would be especially upset.

With nothing better to do than ponder the situation, she decided that, whatever Amelie was doing now, she must have taken up her new habits fairly recently. She couldn't possibly have had such a successful year in sports if she was spending her lunch hours like this! Mikayla could not help feeling like a "peeping Tom" as the boys and girls she was observing paired up and wandered off to secluded areas of the park. She was greatly relieved that a large portion of grass between her and the others was still partially flooded from a heavy rainfall on the weekend; no one was headed in her direction.

Mikayla was further relieved to see that Amelie, who remained seated at the picnic table, maintained some distance between Raymond and herself. His clumsy attempts to draw Amelie to him seemed to be determinedly resisted.

More puzzled than ever, Mikayla had another ten minutes to try and figure out what was going on with Amelie. Mikayla was not completely naive and she certainly understood that trying things out was part of being a teenager. She sometimes felt curious and tempted to experiment herself. But her instincts told her that something was wrong here. Mikayla was sure that what she and Amelie had in common was a love of sports and an understanding of the dedication needed to suceed at them. What could Amelie be thinking?

With her brain bursting with confusion, and her bladder bursting from the failed mission that had sent her into the bush in the first place, Mikayla could only sit absolutely still. As the end of the lunch hour approached, the little Heritage Park gang, as Mikayla had begun to think of them, reassembled at the picnic table. They exchanged a few words, then gradually, and none too steadily, ambled out of the park.

The minute they were out of sight, Mikayla shot out of the bush and sprinted, as best she could under the circumstances, out the opposite end of the park and back to school. She barely made it into the washroom of the empty locker room, then raced to change her clothes and dashed through the door of her homeroom just as the late bell sounded.

Their French teacher started class immediately so there was no opportunity to talk with Victoria. Mikayla acknowledged, with a quick nod, a questioning look from her friend. David, too, shot a curious glance her way. Mikayla realized that she must have looked as flustered and anxious as she felt.

Madame was instructing the class on the format for their upcoming group projects so Mikayla forced herself to pay attention. She would have to wait until later to tell her friends about her noon-time adventure.

* * *

Mr. Daniels was coaching the first long and triple jump practice after school that afternoon. These were popular events and more than thirty students turned out. All pentathlon hopefuls were present as long jump was one of the five events.

"Okay, let's have it. Where were you at lunch?" Victoria demanded as Mikayla was warming up. It was the first chance she'd had all afternoon to find out where Mikayla had disappeared to after morning classes. "David and I looked all over for you so we could plan our group project topic before Madame assigns us one we don't like!"

Mikayla tapped her forehead lightly with the heel of her hand. "Oh my gosh, Tori, I forgot all about that. I'm really sorry. Listen," she lowered her voice, "I'll tell you what happened at lunch, but not now and not here." She looked around for Amelie, who had not yet arrived at the practice.

"What's the big secret?" David and Max asked together as they joined the girls.

"I'll tell you later," replied Mikayla. "I think Coach D. is ready to start."

Victoria took the clipboard from Mr. Daniels and began checking off the names of students who were present. Mikayla felt a moment of sympathy for her friend. Victoria's doctor wouldn't give permission for her to participate in track activities and, in a way, Mikayla was relieved. There was no way she wanted her friend to risk re-injuring herself with summer just around the corner.

Coach Daniels had almost finished his preliminary instructions when Amelie came racing out of the school toward the assembled group. He interrupted himself to make a remark about how even the "stars" were required to show up on time for his practices. Mikayla tensed.

"Sorry, Coach," Amelie said, smiling, as usual. "I was with Mrs. McRae."

Now Mikayla relaxed. If Amelie was seeing Mrs. McRae, the school guidance counsellor, then maybe they were working out whatever it was that was causing her bizarre behaviour. Mikayla certainly hoped so. Competition for the pentathlon aside, Mikayla did not dislike Amelie. Besides, she wouldn't wish today's lunch scene on her worst enemy.

Mikayla knew little about Amelie, mostly what Victoria had shared with her. Amelie and Victoria had met when, representing different elementary schools, they had placed second and third at the Cross Country Championship two years previously. The two girls had hit it off while waiting on the bench to receive their medals. A casual friendship had resumed when Victoria entered grade seven at McClung where Amelie was a year ahead.

Victoria told Mikayla that Amelie's mother had moved east a couple of months ago, following a difficult divorce, to set up a new business and to live closer to her own parents. Amelie and her brother were staying in Ottawa with their father until their mother was ready to have them join her. According to what Amelie had told Victoria, Amelie's mom was not too thrilled about the arrangement because her dad let them "get away with murder," but she'd had no one else to look after them until the school year ended. In a way, knowing all this made Mikayla more sympathetic to Amelie. She could relate to anyone with family problems.

The long jump practice lasted less than an hour and, because there were so many jumpers and only one pit, everyone had only two chances to jump. Distances were not being measured, but it was evident that Mikayla was the most accomplished jumper amongst the girls and could out-jump most of the boys as well. Amelie seemed more like herself than she had the previous afternoon and both her jumps were perfectly executed, although somewhat short of Mikayla's.

After they had changed, Mikayla filled Victoria in briefly on what had happened at the park. As expected, Victoria was upset, mainly because Mikayla's story confirmed what she had already suspected after the throwing-up incident. The two friends spent a few minutes discussing the situation before parting company.

Mikayla met up with David in the schoolyard and they started for home. She hadn't told him anything yet about her mother's visit and it felt good to get her confusion out in the open and talk it over with a friend who cared and seemed to understand. David listened as Mikayla shared her pain about her mother's fading health and her sister's impending adoption.

"At least Ms. Duncan — she's our case worker — says that we'll work out a more regular schedule for Angeline and me to get together," Mikayla told David with relief.

"Hey, maybe I can finally meet this mysterious little sister. Is she as funny-looking as you?" David teased.

Mikayla flashed her friend a phony look of hurt, then quickly returned a playful insult. Amelie Blair and her problems were momentarily forgotten.

8

Frustration and Disappointment

The next two weeks at Nellie McClung Middle School went by in a whirlwind of activity. There were daily track practices, sometimes two a day for pentathletes. The City Relays were coming up in two weeks, the track meet in three, and, for all the grade eight students on the team, there was graduation to prepare for.

As the coach's decision for a pentathlete grew closer, Mikayla's fear of failure increased. She was even beginning to convince herself that she would be happy with running the 400 and doing high jump if Amelie was selected as the pentathlete. It was impossible to tell what Ms. Bradford was going to do. It almost seemed as if she was delaying a decision while keeping both girls working hard to be chosen.

Mikayla had improved her time dramatically in the 800, but Amelie had continued to better her time as well. As expected, Mikayla could not be touched in the long jump or the 100, but Amelie's experience gave her a slight edge in the high jump. High jump seemed to unnerve Mikayla in a way none of the other events did.

Neither girl was particularly adept at shot put, partly because they did not have a great deal of weight on them. Mikayla had good upper body strength, but lacked the specific coordination to execute the skill efficiently. Amelie was supremely coordinated but had no bulk to put behind the shot.

Mikayla had decided to do her extra training for the 800 in the early mornings and in her own neighbourhood. She had no desire to come across Amelie and her friends in Heritage Park again. There were no further incidents with Amelie at practices, although she frequently turned up late, always with a smile and a reasonable excuse.

Victoria had completed her physiotherapy and was given the go-ahead to begin some light training, so she started accompanying Max to his distance practices, running easy laps with lots of stops for stretching. She had become indispensable to the coaches of the various events, but even Victoria had no idea what the plans were for Mikayla and Amelie.

* * *

"Good try, Mik," Victoria called out as Mikayla missed her third attempt at a height that was ten centimetres lower than her best jump.

Pauline shook her head as she addressed Mikayla. "Why can't you just jump the same way each time?"

The inexperienced coach's exasperation showed as she continued, "Every approach is different, sometimes you throw your arms up, sometimes you don't; one jump you look down the bar, next time you don't! Listen, Mikayla, I know we've gone over this before, but let's review it again."

During one practice, Mikayla had successfully cleared a height that was only six centimetres short of the school record. Nevertheless, it seemed as if she was intimidated by the bar and completely unsure of herself.

Now, Mikayla just shrugged. She hated to feel like she was disappointing Pauline, but she had no answers to her coach's questions. Today it didn't help that Amelie was exe-

cuting spectacular jumps in perfect form. Mikayla just got
worse as Amelie got better. After her last miss, Mikayla con-
ferred with Pauline for a few minutes, then sat on the edge of
the stage, continuing to call out support to the other girls.

"Mikayla," Coach Bradford called from the gym door.
"Could I see you for a minute, please, in my office?"

Mikayla stole a worried glance at Victoria as she crossed
the gym floor and followed Ms. Bradford out into the hall.

I guess this is it, Mikayla thought to herself. At least now
I'll know what I'm doing.

After removing a stack of files from the chair, Mikayla sat
down across from her gym teacher and tried a smile. It felt
more like a grimace.

"Well, Mik, how's it going? Are you enjoying your training?" the coach began.

"Great! I really like it and I've learned a lot. I know I still
have a long way to go, especially in high jump and shot put. I
figure next year I should be ready for the pentathlon." Mikayla
couldn't believe she had just said that.

Ms. Bradford raised her eyebrows. "Next year? Don't you
want to do the pentathlon this year?"

"Of course I do!" Mikayla protested. "I guess I just assumed you would pick Amelie. I mean, she's so good at
everything ..." Mikayla trailed off, confused and a little sad to
realize that she'd probably been right in assuming that she
wouldn't be selected.

"Yes, Ammi is a wonderful athlete, isn't she?" Ms. Bradford
paused as if she were considering Amelie's many athletic attrib-
utes. "Mikayla," Ms. Bradford continued, "I know you would
do a great job as our school's pentathlete, but the decision to
enter Ammi in this event has to do with *more* than how good
she is or how good you are. It's not something I can really
discuss with you; you'll have to trust me on this." Ms.
Bradford hesitated before continuing. "Naturally, you'll be

the alternate. I hope you'll continue to train for your events with as much energy and enthusiasm as you've put into preparing for the pentathlon."

Mikayla stood up. "I'll do my best, Coach." It was hard to pretend she didn't care about the decision, even if it hadn't been a surprise.

"And Mikayla," Coach Bradford stood and Mikayla thought she looked just a little sad, too. "You're right. Next year you will definitely be ready."

By the time she returned to the gym, everyone had left except Victoria, who was putting away mats. Victoria took one look at Mikayla and crossed the gym to put her arms around her friend in a comforting hug.

Breaking the embrace, Victoria scowled. "It's really not fair, Mik. You deserve to be the pentathlete more than Ammi does."

"You know, Tori, I didn't really expect to get picked, so why do I feel so disappointed?" Mikayla wondered aloud to her friend.

Victoria pointed out what Mikayla had been thinking. "I guess it's especially hard to take when you know what Ammi's been doing." Victoria frowned, "Mik, what if Ms. Bradford *does* know, and this is just some kind of bribe to straighten her out?"

Mikayla considered Victoria's theory, "I don't think so, Tori. It looks like Ammi has worked things out. Anyway, the decision's been made. I'm just going to have to live with it."

Victoria nodded her head in reluctant agreement.

* * *

That evening Mikayla talked about her disappointment with her foster brother. Jason had failed to make the basketball team in high school the first year he'd gone out for it and he could relate to what she was going through.

"What did you do?" Mikayla asked, imagining how Jason must have felt. Basketball was his life.

"At first," he answered, "I just felt sorry for myself. I really thought I was better than at least two other older guys on the team. I was still growing at that point, and I convinced myself that the coach had overlooked me because I wasn't big enough."

"Yeah, I guess that's kind of what I've been thinking too," Mikayla admitted. "I mean, Amelie *is* older and has more experience."

"Maybe, but the point is, you can't do anything about that; you can only do something about you." Jason paused for a moment, remembering. "What I ended up doing was working harder than ever at the game. I offered to be the team manager so I could work out with them. Then I looked around for a club team to play on. It was too late in the season to make the travel team, but I played house league. I also worked out regularly at the Y to get myself in top condition. Nature kicked in too; I grew. Halfway through the season, the coach moved me up from manager to second string." He shrugged. "The next year I was a starter."

Mikayla considered Jason's experience. She knew she could match his determination but she doubted that she had his talent. Sure, she was a fast sprinter and a decent long jumper, but did she really have what it would take to be a top competitor in the sport she loved so much? The Carrigans had agreed to send her to the Cheetahs Track Club's summer day camp. She supposed that would be a good place to find out if she had any real talent. With that thought, Mikayla made up her mind to continue enjoying her efforts and whatever successes might come her way. Losing out on the pentathlon no longer seemed like the end of the world.

* * *

The next morning Mikayla arrived early at Heritage Park for the middle distance practice. She had already run a warm-up lap and was stretching her legs when her teammates started to enter the park. When Amelie arrived, she approached Mikayla without hesitation.

"Hi, Mik," she began. "I waited around for awhile after high jump yesterday. I thought maybe we should talk about the pentathlon."

Mikayla nodded. She wasn't surprised that Amelie would want to get Coach Bradford's decision out in the open. The more Mikayla trained with Amelie, the more she recognized the older girl's qualities of sincerity and good sportsmanship.

"It's probably just as well we didn't talk right away. I *was* feeling pretty disappointed." She hesitated. "But I'm okay now. Really. You'll do a great job, Ammi, and I'm happy for you."

"Thanks, Mik," Amelie said. "Looks like they're ready to start."

The practice was a tough one. Power running, the coaches called it. Teams of five spaced their runners evenly around the park track. Then the teams ran a continuous relay for fifteen minutes. Depending on how fast a team was, each runner could end up running seven or eight intervals of 120 metres at their fastest speed. It was exhausting, but Mikayla found it was just what she needed. Her last interval was not much slower than her first.

9

The Relays

The day of the Ottawa Relay Championship finally arrived, sunny but cool. The excited runners from McClung gathered in the schoolyard at 6:45 a.m. to await the bus.

"The Relays," as everyone called the event, had been introduced five years previously and was organized by McClung coaches. It had grown in popularity each year and was a perfect lead-up to the larger track and field championships. McClung had dominated the event during the first three years and had come to take their dominance for granted. Last year, however, Hopevale, the other downtown junior high, had handed McClung its first defeat. It had been a narrow victory for Hopevale, and it was felt that this year McClung had the team to regain its "rightful" title.

There were six different relays, and each one had a grade seven and a grade eight division, for a total of twelve races. All the races were coed and runners were limited to participating in two races each.

Victoria, healed at last, and Mikayla, were in one race together, the 4 x 400-metre relay. Mikayla would run the first lap, hopefully establishing a strong lead. David was to receive the baton from her for the second leg and would hand off to Victoria. Van Canh, they hoped, would be their unbeatable anchor runner.

Victoria was also running in the 4 x 200-metre relay, while Mikayla had been assigned as the lead runner in the challenging medley relay in which she would run the first 400, followed by a girl and a boy each running 200, and finishing with a boy, in this case Max, running 800 metres. A second medley relay was set up with a boy running 400 metres and a girl running 800 metres. Mikayla had breathed a sigh of relief when the coaches had put another girl in the 800-metre position.

The grade eight teams were thought to be only slightly weaker than the sevens but, with Amelie running the 400 in one of the medleys and the 800 in the other, those two races were assured of strong finishes.

Since the pentathletes had been announced, Mikayla continued to work hard at all the track practices. She was determined to be at her best when the track meet finally rolled around.

"Mikayla, you're doing too much. You're going to injure yourself!" Victoria had warned. "I don't want you to go through what I did and not be able to participate in the track meet at all!" Swallowing hard, she'd continued, "Do you think maybe you're just trying to prove to everyone that they made the wrong decision by choosing Amelie?"

"No way!" Mikayla had responded vehemently. "I just want to do my best!" Then her voice had softened and she added, "Ammi's been working hard too. She's earned the pentathlon."

* * *

As they waited for the buses to arrive, Mikayla and Victoria were talking excitedly about the relays when Ms. Bradford approached them, a worried look on her face. "Have either of you seen or spoken with Amelie since yesterday afternoon?"

Mikayla shook her head, but Victoria spoke up. "I didn't talk to her but I saw her leave school with Quyen yesterday. The only reason I noticed is because she usually has practice after school and gets picked up by her dad, so I just figured she was taking advantage of some free time to be with her friends."

"Right," Ms. Bradford responded as if talking to herself. "And there were no practices yesterday so she could do just that."

"What's wrong, Coach?" Mikayla inquired. She did not have a good feeling.

"Hopefully nothing, Mik, but Ammi's dad was looking all over for her late yesterday afternoon because she wasn't here when he came to pick her up. I assumed he eventually located her since I didn't hear anything more from him." She surveyed the yard quickly. "But, as you can see, she's not here yet this morning and she didn't say anything about going directly to the track. I thought you girls might know something, but I guess I'd better go phone her house."

Just then two yellow school buses pulled up to the curb. Ms. Bradford indicated that the students should line up and board, before she turned and headed back into the school.

Once seated, Mikayla and Victoria strained to hear Mr. Daniels and Ms. Bradford. The coaches had returned to the bus looking agitated, and they were conversing in hushed tones at the front of the bus.

"Coach B. doesn't look too happy. If she called Amelie and she isn't coming, they must be shifting runners from one race to another," Mikayla whispered.

A few minutes later, the coaches confirmed Mikayla's suspicions when they announced that Irena Malencek, a strong, hard-working runner who lacked natural speed, would take Amelie's positions in the medleys. The other members of Amelie's relay teams grumbled a little while Irena's friends patted her shoulder sympathetically. The students were told only that Amelie was home ill.

* * *

Later that morning, the McClung team got off to a good start with an unexpected second place finish in the grade seven division of the 4 x 100-metre relay. With sixteen teams competing, any placement in the top eight was worth valuable points. The grade eight team managed a fourth place finish. With one event down, McClung was in third place, not a bad position since the school team was not strong in the shorter sprint events.

Mikayla, David, Victoria and Van Canh had been lined up on the infield for their big 4 x 400-metre race. They were all nervous, but showed it in different ways. Van Canh was the only one who appeared calm. He tried to maintain some distance from Mikayla, who was more hyper than her friends had ever seen her. Victoria was quiet, but her fingernails were never very far away from her teeth. David did his best to soothe Mikayla's frazzled nerves.

"Mik," David said, "calm down. There isn't a runner here who can match your time in the 400. You have to stay cool so you don't burn out before the gun goes off!"

His attempts to settle her just seemed to make Mikayla more nervous. "How do *you* know I'm the fastest 400 runner?" she demanded. "Maybe that girl over there from Emily Carr is faster. She looks pretty fast, don't you think?"

It was no use. David surprised Mikayla by leaning over and giving her a light kiss on the cheek.

"That's for luck," he said.

By the time Mikayla had gotten over the unexpected kiss, she and the other starting runners were being led onto the track by the clerk of the course. She was given her lane and listened as the starter began his instructions.

"RUNNERS, TAKE YOUR MARKS."

Mikayla forced herself to relax on the starting line. She recalled Coach Bradford's instructions to rest her eyes a few metres ahead on the track.

"SET."

Mikayla took a deep breath and set her body into the upright starting position. She waited for the sound of the gun.

BANG!

She was off. She was running in lane three and had to remain in that lane for the entire lap. The last three runners of each team would be able to cut to the inside. Suddenly, she had absolutely no fear. Her feet flew in long strides beneath her and she thrilled to the feeling of power in her limbs.

She passed the baton to David fifteen metres ahead of her closest competitor.

David had to work hard to maintain a lead which had dwindled to only a couple of metres by the time he handed off to Victoria.

Victoria seemed unsure of her pace and she was overtaken at the 200-metre mark by one runner and, with only ten metres to go, by yet another.

By the time Van Canh received the baton, the McClung team was behind by almost twenty metres. Catching up looked like an impossibility. Almost effortlessly, Van Canh immediately began to draw even with the second place runner and passed him at the second turn. Down the back straightaway, he continued to gain on the first place runner who panicked and made the mistake of starting his kick too soon. As the two came around the final turn into the last 100, the other runner, out of gas, slowed visibly while Van Canh appeared to actually increase his speed, sailing smoothly across the finish line for the win. He was barely even breathing hard.

Van Canh's teammates ran onto the track and hugged one another joyfully. It was hard to tell if Victoria's were tears of happiness or disappointment over her own performance.

"Thank you so much, V.C.," she sobbed. "We would have lost because of me, but you saved the race!"

David looked at her peculiarly, then responded. "Tori, do you know who that girl is who blew by you halfway around the track?"

Victoria was puzzled by the question. "No, at least I didn't recognize her when she left me in her dust. Why? Who is she?"

"Her name is Heidi Schultz. She goes to Hopevale and trains with the Cheetahs. Her mom was a national team sprinter and Heidi holds the provincial record for her age in the 200 and 400." He glanced at Mikayla. "Don't worry, Mik, she's in a younger age group than you for track."

"How did you know all that?" Mikayla asked incredulously.

"Easy." David grinned. "When I finished my lap, I was standing next to Mr. Daniels whose brain is like a computer for sports facts and records. He was saying, 'Oh, poor Victoria, look who she's up against.' Then he told me all that stuff about Heidi. So you see, your lap was the toughest one."

Victoria finally smiled. "Thanks, David, that makes me feel a lot better. Anyway, you guys were really awesome. What a team!"

As the four friends mounted the first place step of the podium, they waved happily to their friends and teammates in the stands. Standing at the fence were Victoria's parents and older sister. Mikayla gave them a little wave and one to David's father who was also nearby. Van Canh's mother, holding the hands of V.C.'s little twin sisters and smiling broadly, had also come out to cheer on her son. Mikayla scanned the crowd, hoping to catch a glimpse of Jan, Taylor or Jason, but she recognized no one from her foster family in the bleachers or at the fence.

Oh well, she told herself philosophically, maybe they couldn't get away. After all, it's just a little relay meet. And, although she realized that, typically, she had never actually *asked* the Carrigans to come to the meet, she couldn't explain away the lingering feeling of disappointment.

They finished receiving their medals just in time to see the McClung grade eights take third in their 4 x 400-metre race. But Hopevale's grade eight team came in first, so McClung moved up only one place to second. During the next three races, they dropped to fourth, moved up to third, and finally settled back into second place behind Hopevale with only the final medley left to run.

The grade seven team, with Mikayla running the opening 400 and Max running the anchor 800, was the school's strongest team and each athlete ran spectacularly to easily capture first place. The next closest team was 100 metres behind at the finish. The victory moved McClung into first place overall with a three-point margin. They needed only to finish no worse than two places behind Hopevale in the grade eight race and the relay trophy would go back home with them.

Irena Malencek, Amelie's last-minute substitute, was at the start for her 400-metre leg of the race. She was essentially a middle and long distance runner but she was known to give her best effort in everything she did.

As the gun sounded, Mikayla was thinking about the difficulty Irena faced in running a demanding 400 when she had just completed a gruelling 800 only an hour and a half earlier. Suddenly she saw Irena grab her left hamstring as she rounded the second corner going into the back straightaway. Instantly, she was rolling on the track, clutching her leg to her chest and screaming with the burning pain of a badly pulled muscle.

The McClung athletes and coaches were stunned by the misfortune of Irena's accident. Everyone voiced concern for their injured teammate, but they were also disappointed by the outcome of the meet, for they had slid into third place as a result of the final race.

"Poor Irena," Victoria said softly to Mikayla as she rubbed the back of her own recently healed leg. "She was probably just trying to run that lap the way she thought Amelie would do it."

Watching the physiotherapist working over Irena, Coach Daniels just shook his head and wandered dejectedly toward the awards podium to present the meet trophy to Hopevale.

10

The Tables Turn

The buses heading back to McClung were unusually quiet; these were athletes accustomed to victory and post-competition celebrations.

A couple of girls wondered in a whispered conversation how McClung could have lost to "those Hopevale kids" for the second year in a row.

"Don't worry," Max responded, turning around in his seat to interrupt the discussion between the two concerned teammates. "We'll get them next time. Look at all the other sports we've beat them at."

The two girls nodded their heads in agreement.

Victoria leaned toward Mikayla's ear. "Mik," she whispered, "we haven't even had time to figure out what might have happened to Ammi. What do you think?"

Mikayla looked thoughtful. "I don't know," she said finally. "But I sure hope it doesn't have anything to do with the kind of stuff I saw at Heritage Park that day at lunch." She paused, considering, "I've thought a lot about whether I should have told someone about that. You know, for Ammi's own good?"

"It must have been hard not to, Mik, especially after Ms. B. gave the pentathlon to Ammi."

"But maybe she's straightened out, Tori. I mean, she hasn't missed any practices and she just keeps getting better and better," Mikayla puzzled aloud as their bus pulled up alongside the school.

"So do you, Mik," Victoria concluded the conversation. "So do you."

* * *

Inside the school, Victoria and Mikayla were collecting books at their lockers when Coach Bradford approached them.

"Hey, girls, great job at the track today," she smiled.

Victoria beamed, "Thanks, Coach."

Ms. Bradford turned to Mikayla. "Mik, have you got a few minutes? I need to talk to you about something important."

"Sure, Coach," Mikayla answered, then turned to her friend. "Tori, will you tell David I'll be another ten minutes or so? He can go ahead if he's in a hurry."

The girls said goodbye after promises to call that evening and Mikayla followed the coach into her office. She smiled to herself at Ms. Bradford's disorganization as, once again, she had to remove files from the chair in order to sit.

"Mikayla," the coach began, "you were brilliant today. You've left no doubt in my mind that you have a real future in track, provincial level for sure, maybe even national. Will you stay with it?"

"Absolutely, Coach B.!" Mikayla gushed enthusiastically. "I love it. My mom and dad, um, that is, Jan and Taylor, are sending me to the Cheetahs Track Club's summer day camp this year. I can't wait!"

"That's super, Mik," Ms. Bradford responded distractedly. Mikayla could tell that her coach had not called this meeting to dwell on her talents and future plans.

"Mikayla," Ms. Bradford continued, "you know, of course, that Amelie Blair was not able to participate in the relays today."

"Yes, I heard she was sick. What's wrong with her? Is she okay?"

The coach took a deep breath and settled back in her chair before answering. "Mikayla, do you have any idea what's been going on lately with Amelie?"

Uh oh, thought Mikayla, this is going to be serious.

To her coach she responded, "I'm not sure what you're talking about, Ms. Bradford. Do you mean about her mom moving out east and Ammi staying with her dad?" she asked hopefully.

"Well, that's probably part of it, but I'm talking about Amelie herself," she hesitated, "and some of her friends, like Quyen and Raymond. Are you aware of things they might be up to that aren't very good for them?"

Mikayla squirmed in her chair. The coach was more direct. "Listen, Mikayla, this is a strictly confidential conversation we're having. What you say to me, stays with me, unless you give me permission to discuss it with the guidance counsellor."

When Mikayla still said nothing, she continued, "Look, I understand you don't want to get Ammi in trouble, but talking could be the best thing you could do for her."

Mikayla finally responded, "Ms. Bradford, I really don't think I can help you with this. I'm sorry. Is there anything else?"

Coach Bradford regarded Mikayla for several moments.

"Yes, Mik, there's one other thing." She paused. "You are now our pentathlete."

* * *

Mikayla left the school feeling a strange mixture of elation and distress. It was clear from the discussion with Ms. Bradford that Amelie was in serious trouble. Mikayla wondered what could possibly have happened yesterday afternoon to make Ms. Bradford so concerned.

David was sitting on a schoolyard bench reading when Mikayla ran over to him and shared her news. Mikayla was sure he was excited about it, but he kept his cool and shook her hand, saying solemnly, "Mikayla Lamoureux, justice has been done."

They laughed and hugged and started for home. They talked about Amelie, and David said that, in his opinion, anyone who chose to hang out with Raymond Ling was just asking for trouble.

As soon as she walked in the door, Mikayla rushed to the phone and called Victoria. But before she could mention the pentathlon, Victoria burst out, "I just talked to Ammi!"

"Oh my gosh, Tori, what did she say? What happened? Is she all right? Tell me!"

"Well, if you'll stop yapping, I'll tell you," Victoria laughed. "Okay, first of all, the big news is that Ammi is moving out east to her mom's. She's leaving this weekend. Guess what that means?"

"I know what it means, Tori. That's what I was calling to tell you."

"I figured as much," replied Victoria. "Anyway, Ammi told me all this stuff about her past that I never knew before."

"Like what?"

"Like, do you know why Ammi came to McClung in the middle of grade seven last year?"

Before Mikayla could respond, Victoria continued, "She had this huge falling out with all her friends at her old school and they totally rejected her! She didn't tell me what happened and I didn't want to pry."

"You're kidding!" Mikayla cried. "I don't get it. She's probably the most popular girl at McClung!"

"Yeah, you're right," Victoria answered quietly.

"So why has she been hanging out with Raymond Ling and that gang? They could have really messed up her life!"

"Mik ... they practically already did. You can't imagine why she wasn't at the meet today."

"Well, are you going to tell me?"

"Yesterday after school she didn't have any practices ..."

"That's right. No one did. It was supposed to be our rest day before the meet."

"Yep," said Victoria, "but instead of resting, Ammi went off partying with her buddies at Quyen's boyfriend's place. Apparently there was all kinds of stuff there and Ammi ended up passed out in one of the bedrooms."

"No!" cried Mikayla.

"There's more," Victoria went on. "All those so-called friends, except Quyen, took off without even looking for her and she got attacked by some creepy guy!"

"What?"

"Yeah, if it hadn't been for Quyen, well, Ammi *would* have been really hurt," Victoria paused. "Bet you didn't know Quyen has a black belt in Judo."

"Are you serious?"

"Yep. Anyway, I guess Quyen heard Ammi screaming and she came and pulled the guy off her. Actually, Quyen ended up at the bottom of a big pile-up when a bunch of other guys who were still hanging around at the party ran into the room to check out all the noise."

"Tori, I don't know what to say. It's just the worst thing I've ever heard."

"Ammi says she knows she's been stupid, but keeping her friends was really important to her and I guess she thought she had to do everything they did. Anyway," Victoria continued, "somebody called the police because of all the screaming and her dad had to go and pick her up. Obviously, he wouldn't let her go to the meet today. And he's sending her out to her mom's this weekend."

Mikayla, who, at least compared to Victoria, had experienced some fairly rough times in her own young life, was nevertheless aghast at Amelie's story.

"That's so sad, Tori. I had no idea Ammi was so, well, desperate, to hang on to friends who don't even deserve her!"

"Mik," Victoria said gravely, "let's make a solemn vow to always be there for each other and to butt into each other's business if one of us thinks the other is heading for trouble. Okay?"

"Definitely," responded Mikayla, but to herself she wondered if *anyone* could really keep a promise to always be there for her. It was something she had never experienced before.

11

Good News and Bad News

The next day, the entire school was talking about Amelie and Quyen's escapades. Raymond was claiming that he'd had no idea Amelie was still in the house. No one actually knew the real story, but that did not prevent the rumours from spreading.

Mikayla was surprised when Quyen approached her at lunchtime and handed her a sealed envelope. "It's from Ammi," she said. "She asked me to give it to you."

"When did you see her?" exclaimed Mikayla.

"Her dad brought her by last night to see how I was doing. Pretty cool, eh?" she boasted, pointing at a bruised and swollen left eye. "Anyway," Quyen continued, serious again, "she gave me this letter for you and said it was really important."

"Thanks," Mikayla responded, then added quietly, "Quyen, I heard about how you helped Ammi out. *That's* really cool."

"It was nothing," answered Quyen. "Ammi's my friend." With that, she turned and headed down the hall.

Mikayla moved off toward the gym. Pauline would be in shortly for high jump practice, but right now Mikayla was just looking for some privacy so she could read Amelie's letter. She crossed the floor to the stage and hoisted herself up.

Sitting on the edge with her legs dangling, she carefully opened the envelope and pulled out two sheets of blue paper. She read:

> *Hey Mik,*
>
> *I've been wanting to talk to you for a while but the time never seemed quite right. I've been wanting to tell you what a great athlete I think you are! But you always seem disappointed in yourself. I see that because I felt that way about myself too. No matter how often people would tell me I was really good at something, I always thought they were just trying to make me feel better. Even when I won medals, I would say it was just "luck." But ever since I've been training for the pentathlon with you, I started to figure out that, if you are awesome (and you are), then I must not be so bad myself. After all, even though you could beat me at some things, I was beating you at others (not by much though)! So, thanks for helping me believe in myself a little, even if you didn't know you were doing it!*
>
> *Anyway, I guess Tori probably told you what happened yesterday. Pretty pathetic, eh? I hope you guys won't waste time with so called friends who help you get in trouble and then take off just when you need them (not including Quyen, of course)!*

Mikayla paused in her reading, absorbing the message. She turned to the second page.

> *There's just one more thing I want to tell you. I know how hard you've worked on your 800 and it must be frustrating that you couldn't beat me. Well, you might have soon — you were getting really close! Next week you'll be running the pentathlon 800 at the track meet.*

The girl you'll be competing against from Queen Victoria is Jessie Tremaine. She used to be my best friend before I came to McClung. I have never beaten her in the 800. But you can. YES, YOU CAN! You just have to remember this: Jessie likes to go out fast and set the pace. You've got to stay with her for that first lap and it will feel comfortable to you because it's almost as fast as you run a 400. She tries to wear out her competition with a fast first lap but she always has enough left to run a fairly good second lap while everyone else is dying. With all the training you've been doing, you can run a great second lap too. Trust me, you can beat her, and I hope you do. She really hurt me once. It's no big deal anymore, but if I can't be there to win that race, I wish you would!

Well, Mik, it's too bad we didn't get to know each other better. We might have been good friends! I know I'll miss training with you. Good luck next week (even though you won't need much). I'll be thinking about all of you. Please write and let me know how it goes. Tori has my mom's address. Bye for now.

Ammi

Mikayla sat motionless for several moments. She was strangely moved by this letter from a girl she had hardly known who was willing to extend her support at a time when she must have been feeling pretty low herself. She folded the letter and tucked it back into the envelope just as Pauline and the other high jumpers entered the gym.

The practice was a tough one. Pauline put the girls through a rigorous warm-up and stretch and she fussed and played with each of their approaches. Everyone jumped well, but Mikayla out-jumped even Quyen. Her final jump was higher than anything she had ever cleared before.

* * *

The level of excitement at the school increased dramatically the following week as the track meet neared. There were over eighty-five McClung students, almost a quarter of the student population, either competing in the meet or assisting with officiating.

Easy practices were held on Monday and Tuesday. On Wednesday, the athletes were ordered to rest so they would be ready and refreshed for the meet on Thursday and Friday.

That evening, Mikayla sat at the Carrigan supper table chatting excitedly with Jason about the events she would be participating in the next day. Jan and Taylor were debating the merits of a new Italian film they had seen the weekend before. It was a fairly typical scene in the Carrigan home at supper-time and it was Mikayla's favourite time with her family.

When the phone rang, the intrusion silenced everyone momentarily. Jan answered and passed the phone to Mikayla.

"For you, Mik. Ms. Duncan."

As Mikayla took the phone, everyone excused themselves so she could speak in privacy.

"Hello, Ms. Duncan. How are you?" Mikayla felt a pang of guilt at her hope that the social worker was not phoning to set up another visit with her mother. Not now, she silently wished, just wait until after the track meet.

"I'm fine, Mikayla, thank you. You're well, I hope?"

"Yes, ma'am, I'm fine."

"Mikayla ..." she hesitated so long Mikayla thought maybe she hadn't heard her response. "Mikayla," she began again, "you haven't by any chance heard from your mother, have you?"

"No, Ms. Duncan, I haven't talked to her since the last time she was here with you and Angeline. Why? Is anything the matter?" Mikayla heard panic in her own voice.

"I don't think so, dear. It's just that she checked out of her nursing home for the day yesterday morning and she hasn't returned yet. The staff there contacted me this morning and I've been trying to locate her, you know, checking some of the places she goes, talking to people who know her ..." Ms. Duncan trailed off. "I just thought she might have tried to reach you."

Mikayla tried to remain calm. "Well, she hasn't ... do you think something has happened to her ... what are you going to do? What can *I* do?" It all came out in a rush and Mikayla was grateful when her foster mother appeared in the kitchen doorway with a look of concern on her face.

"Mikayla, listen to me," urged Ms. Duncan, "there's probably nothing to worry about. This has happened before but she's always turned up." Again she hesitated. "Mikayla, phone me immediately if you hear from her. You have my home number?"

"Yes, Ms. Duncan," Mikayla answered weakly.

"And, Mikayla, I know it's easier said than done, but try not to worry. I'm certain she will show up soon. Do you want me to speak with Jan or Taylor?"

"No, it's okay. I'll let them know what's happening. Please call me as soon as you hear anything."

They said goodbye. With only a few accompanying tears, Mikayla related the story of her mother's disappearance to her foster family. Jan and Taylor tried, without success, to discourage Mikayla from attending the track meet the following day if her mother was still missing.

"I need something to keep me busy," whispered Mikayla. "My staying home won't help find my mother. I would rather just come home from the meet tomorrow and find out that everything is all right."

Mikayla excused herself early and went to her room to make sure everything was ready for the meet. Feeling strangely detached, she went about her preparations automatically, not allowing herself to dwell on the recent development.

When Janice Carrigan went into Mikayla's room a half hour after the distressed girl had left the family, Mikayla was sound asleep, her track clothes neatly folded at the foot of the bed.

12

Day One at the Track

Early the next morning in the schoolyard, Victoria approached Mikayla and David who were sitting in silence with their backs against the wall of the school.

"Hey, David, Mik. What's up?" Victoria ventured.

Mikayla looked up blankly. "Huh? Oh … Listen, you guys, I'm just trying to focus my energies here. I'm probably not going to be very good company today, so …" she trailed off and looked back down at her hands resting in her lap. Mikayla made no further efforts to talk, so David stood up.

"Okay, Mik, we'll leave you alone, if that's what you want." David made the statement into a half-question but, getting no response from Mikayla, he and Victoria wandered away.

Mikayla was vaguely aware that her friends were probably talking about her as they moved off but, at the moment, she could not summon the energy to reassure them. It was all she could do to focus her concentration on the pentathlon events of the day. She was determined to keep the question of her mother's whereabouts tucked away in a corner of her mind.

* * *

The Terry Fox track was situated next to Mooney's Bay Beach. A big hill, which was used as the final approach for the cross-country course, separated the two locations. The McClung students were boisterous and full of good spirits as their bus turned into the parking lot of the vast sport and recreation complex. Theirs was one of the first buses to arrive; they had their pick of the seats in the bleachers, although few of them would actually spend a great deal of time there. Walking around the athletic facility and meeting new people was one of the highlights of the two-day meet. School pride and spirit made students fiercely loyal to their own team, but that didn't mean that there couldn't be kids worth meeting from other schools.

As the starting time for the meet drew nearer, the track and bleachers became filled with hundreds of athletes in school colours, some making an effort at serious warm-ups, others just milling around enjoying the increasing level of excitement. All the activity had perked Mikayla up and she was sitting with her friends in the stands when the gun fired to start the bantam girls' 1500-metre race. The announcer called for the intermediate boys and girls to report to the starting line for instructions, and Mikayla managed a smile at Max as Victoria took his hand to help him up. Everyone wished him good luck.

Before long, it was time for Mikayla to start warming up for the pentathlon high jump. All the pentathletes had been gathered together to meet each other and receive instructions on the schedule of their events.

Mikayla chatted for a few minutes with Bonnie Tam, who was from Hopevale and was the only pentathlete in the group Mikayla knew.

"Do you understand how the scoring works?" Mikayla asked.

"Well, there are twelve of us competing," Bonnie responded. "The first place finisher in each event will get twelve points, second place, eleven points, and so on. Trophies will go to the girl and guy who get the highest total score."

"Oh," replied Mikayla, "*that's* why my coaches told me to go for the best place finish I could manage in each event instead of just worrying about winning."

Bonnie nodded her agreement.

Now Mikayla understood that if she finished, say, second and third in every event, she could still be the overall winner as long as one or two other girls did not dominate the top two spots.

Mikayla was as friendly with the other competitors as she was able to be, under the circumstances, but she did not go with Bonnie to join any of the smaller groups now stretching in preparation for the high jump. This event, more than any of the other four she would be participating in, required tremendous concentration, focus and determination, all of which might prove difficult today.

After winning her 200-metre heat, Victoria joined David, Max and several other friends at the bleachers overlooking the high jump pit. Mikayla gave a halfhearted little wave in their direction as she and her fellow pentathletes readied themselves for their first jumps.

Her friends looked on as Mikayla barely cleared the warm-up height and then struggled to establish a starting mark and an approach that would propel her successfully over the fibreglass bar.

Mikayla was vaguely aware that the thirty minutes or so it took her to eliminate herself from the high jump competition were probably painful for her friends to watch. She cleared the first height on her second attempt, but took three tries to get over the second height. The next height produced three jumps from Mikayla that weren't even close. The bar was a full twenty centimetres below the best jump Mikayla had done in practice only one week earlier when she had jumped so well against Quyen.

The only consolation for Mikayla was that four other girls had already been eliminated at the previous height and it looked like two more could go out at this one. The best she could hope to finish in this event was sixth, but eighth was more likely. Five points, she thought miserably, and seven other girls already ahead of me! One of them was Amelie's former friend, Jessie Tremaine.

"Well, Mik, you sure weren't yourself out there this morning. What went wrong?" It was Coach Bradford, resting a sympathetic hand on Mikayla's shoulder as the disappointed girl picked up her sweats and water bottle.

"I don't know, Coach," Mikayla responded honestly. "I just couldn't get focused. I let myself get psyched out by all the talent."

"And you forgot that you'd brought along a little talent of your own?" the coach pressed.

"It just didn't feel right. I couldn't get my approach and my legs felt heavy." She paused. "Sorry, Coach. I know you thought I'd do better."

"Don't be sorry on my account, Mikayla. It didn't work out the way we might have liked, but it's over now. Time to move on and forget about high jump. The 100 is coming up just before lunch. Shake this one off and psych yourself up for speed." She smiled, "Now why don't you go over and try to cheer up that sorrowful-looking bunch of friends of yours over there."

Mikayla walked toward her friends with a sheepish expression on her face. "Guess I didn't provide a lot of entertainment for the 'peanut gallery,' did I?"

Her friends smiled at the use of one of Ms. Bradford's favourite expressions. It was a good way to get through an awkward moment and Mikayla was then able to accept her friends' support. Everyone agreed that things would improve. The good news, as they headed back toward the stands, was the announcement that Victoria had qualified for the 200-metre final.

Mikayla walked beside Victoria.

"Sorry about this morning, Tori," she apologized. "I've had a lot on my mind lately."

"Don't worry about it, Mik; I know you've been under some pressure. You've got to try and relax, though," Victoria urged, "so you can do what you came here to do."

The girls settled in a shady spot on the grass near the track. Their friends had split off, some to the concession stand, others to warm-up areas to prepare for events.

"I guess," Mikayla replied softly. Then, with genuine enthusiasm, she added, "Hey! Congratulations on your 200! You're doing great! Right about now, I wish I was doing only events I like instead of the stupid pentathlon. I was crazy to want to do it. Those other girls are all so good!"

Victoria looked squarely at her friend and replied, "Mikayla, you wanted this event, you worked your butt off for this event, and you're going to give this event everything you've got. No more 'I can't' or 'I'm not good enough' or 'everyone else is better.' No more!"

Mikayla was taken aback by her friend's outburst, but she understood what Victoria was trying to do and was grateful that her friend would risk looking her in the eye to deliver the tough message she needed. The exchange boosted Mikayla's confidence.

On the track, the senior boys' 200-metre heats were finally finishing. The announcer called for the pentathlon boys and girls to report to the 100-metre starting line.

"Good luck, Mik," Victoria said, giving Mikayla a quick hug. "Don't forget, bud, this event is yours." Pointing an accusing finger at her departing friend, she yelled, "Go for it!"

Mikayla was feeling better than she had since the previous evening's phone call. The light of day and the warmth of her friends' support had dulled her fears for her mother and she felt suddenly that everything would be all right.

When the pentathletes arrived at the starting line, brief instructions were given and the girls were organized into two heats. Mikayla would be running in heat 2, lane 4. The other five girls running with her were holding first, third, fifth, ninth and eleventh places from the high jump. Mikayla had ended up seventh. She knew she needed a first in the 100 to stay in contention.

Looking down the track toward the finish line as the first heat went to their starting positions, Mikayla was stunned to see her mother, her real mother, Noelle, leaning up against the low fence that separated the bleachers from the track. She was a long distance away, more than 100 metres, but Mikayla was certain it was her. The woman appeared to be looking around and Mikayla stood and waved her arms to try and draw her attention.

At the sound of the gun, Mikayla's attention snapped back to the track ahead where six of her competitors were driving with everything they had toward the finish line. Her eyes never left their backs until she saw them pull up at the end of their race. From where she was, it was difficult to determine the order of finish, but it looked to Mikayla like Amelie's old friend, Jessie Tremaine, who had taken fourth place in the high jump, was the easy winner of that heat. She'd have to wait until her own run was over to find out how everyone else had placed and how the times from the two heats compared.

Mikayla immediately returned her focus to where she thought she had seen her mother and was relieved to see her still standing there, still looking around. As Mikayla and the other runners in her heat moved up to the starting line, she thought her mother caught sight of her. She tried waving again and was disappointed when her mother didn't return the greeting. But her disappointment gave way to elation that her mother had come out to see her participate in the meet. Mikayla wondered, only fleetingly, how her mother knew about the meet and where to come and how she'd had the good luck to show up at the perfect time!

It doesn't matter how she found out, Mikayla said to herself happily, only that she's here and she's safe and …

Mikayla realized suddenly — and just in time — that the starter was about to fire his gun. She took her customary start position and responded instantaneously to the sound of the gun, focusing every last bit of energy on the task at hand. She felt the exhilarating power in her legs and arms as they pumped efficiently to drive her down the track toward the finish line. Her peripheral vision initially allowed her to see the girls running in the lanes on either side of her. By the time she had completed twenty-five metres, however, she could no longer see anyone in the other lanes. Incredibly, she had not achieved full speed yet and, by fifty metres, she knew she would win easily.

Mikayla was in her own universe now, where, despite the loud cheering coming from the stands, she heard only silence, punctuated by the sound of her own heartbeat and forceful breathing. It was not until she crossed the finish line that the sounds of the world around her came back in a rush. The timer from her lane took hold of her arm, congratulating her on her run and confirming her name and school.

A moment later, Victoria was at her side, laughing and shouting, "You did it, Mik! Man, did you ever do it. You ran a 12.9. That's one-tenth of a second off the intermediate girls' 100-metre record!"

"But is it a faster time than the first heat?" Mikayla wondered aloud.

"Didn't you hear me, Mik?" Victoria replied. "You almost broke an eleven-year-old record! The winning time in the first heat was something like 14.0. The next best time in yours was 13.8!"

"My mom!" Mikayla cried, startling Victoria, who was still trying to make her friend understand what she had just accomplished.

Mikayla strained to look over the heads of the runners and officials milling about on the track. Her mother was no longer standing where she'd been only moments earlier.

"What are you doing, Mik? Did you see Jan?" asked a bewildered Victoria.

"No, my mom, my *real* mom! She was standing right over there just before my race began. You didn't see her?"

"Mik," said Victoria, laying a calming hand on Mikayla's shoulder, "I've never met your mother." Helplessly, she added, "I'm sorry, Mik, I don't even know what she looks like."

"Let's go, Tori. Help me find her." Mikayla grabbed Victoria by the hand and headed toward the stands. The fact that she had just come close to a city record was the furthest thing from her mind.

The two girls spent the next half-hour searching the athletic facility grounds for Noelle. Mikayla was frantic at first, but eventually calmed down as it became clear that her mother was nowhere to be found.

"Maybe it was just someone who *looked* like your mom," suggested Victoria, after the girls had finished searching the beach area. "Are you sure it was her?"

Mikayla looked uncertain. "I *thought* I was sure but now, I'm not sure of anything!" She paused for a moment. "Come on, let's get back to the track."

As the girls walked through the entrance to the track area, Max ran up to them, out of breath. "Tori, where have you been? They've already made the second call for your 200 final. David and V.C. have been warming up for the last fifteen minutes!"

"Oh my gosh," panicked Victoria, "I completely forgot! I'll see you later, Mik," she called over her shoulder, running off toward the infield.

"Sorry, Tori. Thanks for your help and, good luck!" Mikayla yelled through her hands to the quickly departing back of her friend.

Now Mikayla worried that her friend, having no time to stretch before her race, would injure herself again and it would be all Mikayla's fault for being so selfish.

* * *

Fortunately, Tori not only finished the race safely, but spectacularly, with a final burst of speed that resulted in the finish judges being unsure of who had actually won. In a most unusual occurrence, the timers for the two lanes had watches that displayed identical results, right down to the hundredths of a second. A back-up watch on lane one provided such a similar result that the meet convenor decided to declare both girls gold medalists. Van Canh also took the gold medal in the 200 and David finished a strong third to capture the bronze.

Mikayla was, of course, thrilled for her friends and especially relieved that no harm had come to Victoria. When Victoria mounted the podium, however, Mikayla again felt envious as she witnessed the pride on the faces of Victoria's parents and sister watching their youngest family member receive her medal. The process repeated itself when David's and Van Canh's parents looked on as their sons were presented with awards.

It only increased Mikayla's own sense of inadequacy to see what Victoria had managed to achieve in such a short time compared with how poorly she, herself, had done after so much preparation. Mikayla did not know how to come to terms with all the confusion she felt. The unexpected sighting of her mother, followed by her sudden and inexplicable disappearance, did nothing to boost Mikayla's morale and confidence.

It was in this state of mind that Mikayla made her way to the long jump pit to warm up for an event in which — she knew from past success — she excelled. Her first task was to try and clear her mind enough to concentrate on setting up the approach. After a couple practice jumps and adjustments to her take-off marker, Mikayla made a clean, though hardly spectacular, jump to complete her allotted warm-up.

There, she said to herself, that felt better. I think I've got the approach down now. Mikayla sat on the grass beside the jumping area and stretched her legs while the rest of the pentathletes finished their warm-up jumps. She spotted her friends, who had completed their events for the day, crossing the infield to watch her compete.

"Congratulations, guys," Mikayla called to them. "Let's see those medals."

Van Canh still wore the gold medal around his neck. Grinning with pride, he leaned down so Mikayla could take a closer look. Victoria and David had already stashed their medals away in gym bags.

"Cool, V.C.," said Mikayla and held up her hand for a high-five.

The long jump official called the participants down to the starting area. Mikayla's three friends offered their biggest smiles and words of encouragement to her as she made her way to where the others were already gathered.

Mikayla was on the list as the fourth jumper, determined by the position she now held overall in the pentathlon as a result of her success in the 100. Each girl would now take three jumps in turn, with only their best jump counting in the final standings of the event.

Mikayla continued to stretch while the first three girls jumped. When her name was called, she approached her mark, having already decided that her first attempt would be conservative. She wanted to have at least one good jump under her belt before going for broke.

She took a little skipping step with her left foot and quickly came up to speed, focusing on the narrow strip of wood just before the sand pit. As she neared it, Mikayla realized that, unless she did some fast shuffling of her feet, she was going to overshoot the take-off board, faulting on her first attempt. Instead, she took off on the opposite foot, several centimetres short of the board. The result — 3.87 metres — would have been considered quite a good effort by most of the girls competing. For Mikayla, who regularly jumped over four metres in practice, it was mediocre. Nevertheless, it was a clean jump and it counted. Mikayla relaxed a little and rejoined her friends while the rest of the field completed the first round.

"I'm having a little trouble finding my start," Mikayla lamented to her friends.

"Yeah," replied David, "looks like you need to move it back a half a step. You want to take off on your right foot, eh?"

"Um hmm," Mikayla responded thoughtfully. "But no matter where I put it, I can't seem to hit the board."

"Sure you can, Mik!" Victoria piped in enthusiastically. "You're up again after the next girl."

Mikayla gave her friend a weak smile and made her way down to the starting area. She found her mark and moved it back several centimetres after the girl ahead of her started down the runway. She was determined to go hard on this jump and, at the go-ahead signal from the official, she shot down the runway, hit the board perfectly and flew through the air stretching her feet out toward the end of the pit. She knew while still airborne, however, that her body was off balance, the weight of her upper body was not far enough over her legs. She desperately tried to throw herself forward before landing but her feet touched down and she was forced to drop her hands behind to catch herself. The jump, when measured as required from the furthest point back - - her hand prints — was a mere 3.38 metres.

Currently, the leading jumps were 4.11, 4.06 and 3.93. Mikayla's 3.87 was fourth best. At the beginning of the third round, Bonnie Tam amazed the other competitors and the crowd with a clean jump of 4.18 metres. Mikayla had competed against Bonnie previously, and she was certain she could out-jump the Hopevale athlete.

Mikayla took her time preparing for her final jump, trying to tune out her surroundings. She focused determinedly on her objective. Her approach was strong, her take-off felt good and her form in the air was practically flawless. Therefore it was with horror that she heard the official yell out "FAULT!" just as her feet landed in the sand.

"What do you mean?" she asked with alarm, while trying to shake the sand out of her shoes.

The official motioned her over to the take-off board where she could see the print of the toe of her shoe in the smooth, damp sand that lay flush with the board. It was undeniable proof that she had stepped over the legal take-off point.

"Sorry, Mikayla, it was a great jump, too, 4.41," said the supervising teacher as he knelt and smoothed the sand in preparation for the next jumper.

Dejected, Mikayla saw the sympathy in the eyes of her friends as they stood away from the jumping area and waited for her to join them. Both David and Victoria offered her a ride home with their parents so she wouldn't have to ride the school bus, but she declined, saying that she had to go back to the school anyway for a forgotten book. The fact of the matter was, she simply couldn't handle any more pity.

13

Going from Bad to Worse

The McClung track team was surprisingly subdued on the bus ride back to the school. They had experienced phenomenal success at the meet and were currently first in the overall standings. A decent showing on the second day would ensure them another in a long line of city championships. But a combination of fatigue and the effects of the day's high heat and humidity had rendered even the most high-strung amongst them wilted and exhausted.

Mikayla, alone in one of the back row seats, drifted in and out of sleep as the bus, caught in rush hour traffic, bumped along through road construction zones.

Thank God, she thought, it's over for today. The troubled girl would have found it difficult, if not impossible, to face another running or jumping event that day. She was only grateful that her friends had been there to support and encourage her, despite what she considered to have been almost total failure on her part. Mikayla was certain that her coaches would now regret having entered her in the pentathlon. The worst part was not really understanding what had gone wrong. She closed her eyes again and began another painful review of the afternoon, but sleep overtook her thoughts before long.

When Mikayla awoke, the bus had finally cleared the construction area and was now only a few minutes away from

McClung. She looked up to see Ms. Bradford moving down the aisle toward her.

"Hi, Mikayla," she said, stopping at Mikayla's seat, but making no move to sit down. "How're you doing?"

"I'm okay, Coach," Mikayla responded, not altogether truthfully.

"You know you're not out of this, don't you, Mik? I mean, you still have two more events. Right now there are only seven points between you and the leader ..."

"Right, seven points and four girls between me and first place," Mikayla interrupted in a discourteous tone of voice she had never before used with her coach. She was immediately sorry. "I apologize, Ms. Bradford. It just feels like nothing's going right. No matter how hard I try, I keep blowing everything!"

Mikayla's coach sat down in the seat ahead of Mikayla's. "Mik," she said, looking at the forlorn girl compassionately. "Have you already forgotten about the results of the 100-metre run? You almost broke a record!"

Mikayla looked up, startled. "I did?"

"You mean you didn't know?" Ms. Bradford asked with surprise.

"Well, I guess I knew that I had the best time, but ..." She hesitated before continuing, "Well, there was something else going on that kind of distracted me."

Mikayla saw that Ms. Bradford was about to pursue the subject and was relieved that the bus was just pulling up alongside the school.

"We'll talk some more tomorrow morning, Mik," said Ms. Bradford, standing up. "Get a good night's sleep, okay?"

"Sure, Ms. B., no problem," Mikayla answered, offering up a little smile to reassure her coach.

She waited until the rest of the students had cleared off the bus, then Mikayla gathered her belongings and moved slowly down the aisle to the door. "Thanks," she said automatically to the driver, and descended the steps to the sidewalk.

Hearing the insistent honk of a car horn, Mikayla peered around the front of the bus and saw the Carrigan family car parked across the street. Ms. Duncan was standing in the street next to the back door of the automobile, waving at Mikayla and motioning her to come over.

Minutes earlier, Mikayla would not have believed the day could get any worse, but the scene before her indicated news that was not likely to be welcome. She waited for a car to pass, then proceeded slowly toward her social worker.

"My mother, she's ..."

"She's in the hospital, Mikayla, we're taking you to see her now," Ms. Duncan responded, reassuringly.

Mikayla climbed into the back seat, followed by Sarah Duncan, and dropped her gym bag on the floor of the car. Taylor was driving and Jan sat in the passenger's seat, her head turned toward Mikayla with a worried expression.

"Will somebody please tell me what's going on with my mother?" Mikayla implored.

"Mikki," Jan began, "we don't have the whole story yet, but this is what we *do* know. Ms. Duncan received a call late this morning from the hospital. Your mother had been brought in by ambulance earlier following a 911 call."

"But who called? Where was she? What happened to her?" The questions came tumbling out of Mikayla's mouth as she looked from one person to the next, waiting for answers.

Sarah Duncan took control of the discussion. "Apparently, the 911 call was made by a friend of your mother's who she often visits. From what I understand, Noelle was at this friend's apartment when the call was made." The social worker turned to face Mikayla squarely and continued. "Your mother was terribly ill when she arrived at emergency. It was a rough morning for her, Mikayla, but it seems they've stabilized her for now. It's hard to predict what will happen but I'm sure the doctors looking after her will have a better idea by the time we arrive."

"I don't understand why no one came for me this morning at the track. You knew where I was!" Mikayla cried out accusingly.

"Mik," Jan responded gently, "it took some time for the hospital to sort out the details of who your mother was, where she lived and who to contact. When she first arrived at the hospital, they had their hands full just dealing with her medical condition. By the time Sarah was contacted and reached me, it was mid-afternoon. I called Taylor and waited for him to come home from school and, as soon as he did, we went out to the track. Unfortunately, the bus had left just a few minutes before we arrived."

Mikayla, calmer now, apologized, "I'm sorry, Jan, I didn't mean to …"

"It's all right, Mik," Jan smiled warmly, "I'm sure it's been very difficult for you since Sarah phoned last night. I just hope you managed to have a good day."

Mikayla tried to return Jan's smile as she considered her miserable day. She welcomed the sight of the hospital's emergency entrance.

"Now, Mikayla," Ms. Duncan warned, "your mother is in intensive care. Visits are limited to just a few minutes." She took Mikayla gently by the elbow after they had exited the car and were moving through the parking lot. "Mikki," she added, coming to a stop in order to get Mikayla's full attention, "your mother is very ill. She will probably not even look as well as she did the last time you saw her a few weeks ago."

Mikayla thought about the last time she had seen her mother, how thin and grey she had appeared. She understood that Ms. Duncan was trying to prepare her for something even worse. Mikayla shivered despite the extreme heat of the late spring day.

They entered the hospital and were directed to the intensive care unit. At the nurses' station, Sarah Duncan introduced Mikayla to the duty nurse. The young man, who had been reviewing patient charts, glanced at Mikayla briefly and pushed a button on the console in front of him. "I don't have time to help you right now," he said cooly. "You'll have to wait for someone from the ward." He then returned his attention to the clipboard in front of him. After a few minutes, a nursing assistant emerged and came directly up to them.

She looked around at the adults but then directed her greeting to Mikayla. "You must be Mrs. Lamoureux's daughter," the woman said. She was an imposing figure, close to six feet tall and massive in a strong, solid way. Her skin was very dark and her hair was very short, but it was her eyes that caught and held Mikayla's attention. The deep brown irises, sparkling against a background of pure white, were the kindest, most understanding eyes Mikayla had ever seen.

"Yes, I am," Mikayla responded weakly. "I'm one of her daughters. My name is Mikayla."

"Mikayla. That's a pretty name. Mine's Louanne. Now let's go see your mother." And she led Mikayla by the hand down the hall.

"What do you know about your mother's condition, Mikayla?" asked Louanne softly, pausing at the door to the unit.

"Nothing, really," Mikayla responded, then paused for a moment before adding, "I mean, I know her heart is bad. Did she have another heart attack?"

"Something like that. She's putting up a good fight, but ..." Louanne trailed off as she saw the doctor approaching. "Here's Dr. Soo. She'll fill you in."

Before going in to see her mother, Mikayla listened as the young resident explained that her mother's condition was critical. Mikayla nodded dumbly at the doctor, still not fully realizing the seriousness of what she was hearing.

Louanne pushed opened the door and Mikayla followed the doctor into the darkened ward. They stopped at a bed in which Mikayla saw the frail ghost of the woman who was her mother. An oxygen mask covered her nose and mouth and she was hooked up to what Mikayla assumed to be life-support machines. In addition, there were two intravenous tubes leading to needles in her arms. Noelle's eyes were closed but they fluttered when Mikayla touched her cheek softly.

"Mama," Mikayla whispered close to her mother's ear, "can you hear me?"

The eyes remained closed but the woman's lips parted and Mikayla heard, as quietly as a sigh, the feeble voice of her mother's answer, "Mikki?"

"Yes, Mama, it's me." Mikayla kept her lips near her mother's ear, speaking softly and soothingly. Teardrops glistened on her eyelashes.

Noelle's body seemed to become more alert; gradually her eyes opened slightly and tried to focus on her daughter's face, bent close over her own.

"Baby, I want ... I need to ... to tell you something," Noelle Lamoureux said to her daughter.

"No, Mama, don't say anything. Just rest and get better," Mikayla pleaded.

But Noelle was determined. "Help me ..." She was struggling to remove the oxygen mask. Getting a brisk nod from the doctor, Mikayla slid it down so her mother could speak more easily. "Mikki, you ... you've got to let me talk," she whispered fiercely. "Just listen now, do you hear?"

Mikayla simply nodded and didn't attempt to stop the tears as they dropped from her lashes.

Noelle fixed her eyes on her daughter's. "Baby ... you dry those tears ... you've got to stay strong ... you're the only one ..." Noelle faltered for a moment, mumbling something Mikayla could not understand.

After a short silence, filled only with Noelle's laboured breathing, she continued. "You are the only one, Mikki ... the only one who can make your dreams come true ... no one else can do that for you ... you've got to be strong ... and, baby, don't you ever forget ... your mama loves you, Mikki ... your mama ..."

Mikayla listened hard but couldn't make out anything else. She put the mask back in place, allowing her mother to breathe more easily as she seemed to drift off. She watched her mother's face relax and looked in alarm to the doctor who told her that her mother was merely sleeping.

Mikayla turned back to Noelle and whispered softly in her mother's ear, "I love you, too, Mama. Angie and I both love you."

The doctor's beeper sounded and she excused herself, saying she'd meet Mikayla at the nurses' station in a few minutes. Louanne checked Noelle's IVs and monitors, then gently took Mikayla by the hand to lead her toward the door.

"You know, Louanne," Mikayla said. "Earlier today, I was positive I saw Mama at my track meet. It looked so much like her, but I was pretty far away. I guess it couldn't have been her ... could it?"

Louanne stopped and stared for a moment at the young girl standing beside her in such a state of sorrow and helplessness. "I don't think so, Mikayla. Why, what time was it you thought you saw her?"

"Well, it would have been just before lunch time. That's when I ran my 100," Mikayla replied.

Again, Louanne hesitated before responding. "Mikayla, I don't know if anyone was planning to tell you this but ... at half past eleven this morning your mother went into cardiac arrest. We lost her. Those doctors worked hard to bring her back." Now Louanne looked directly into Mikayla's eyes and held them with her own. "Only the good Lord knows where she went for those few minutes she left us."

Mikayla, shaken, followed Louanne out of the room and back down the hall to where the Carrigans, Sarah Duncan and Dr. Soo were conferring in low voices at the nurses' station. Jan glanced up as they approached and her face registered concern at Mikayla's appearance.

Jan walked forward to meet Mikayla and put her hands on the girl's shoulders. "Are you all right, Mikki?"

Mikayla blinked and shook her head slightly as if to clear it. "Yeah, I'm okay," she replied.

Wrapping a protective arm around Mikayla, Jan said to the others, "I think she's been through enough today. Let's get her home."

She turned to Mikayla and said soothingly, "Mik, how about some supper and a good sleep? You look exhausted. We'll come back to see your mother first thing tomorrow morning."

Mikayla just nodded dumbly and, for a moment, made no response. Suddenly, she looked at Jan and said softly, but with resolve, "I can't come back in the morning. I've got to do something tomorrow. Something my mom would understand." She turned to Taylor, "Would you bring me to see her after the meet?"

"Of course, Mikayla," Taylor replied.

With her back to Dr. Soo, Mikayla could not see the young doctor shake her head sadly at the Carrigans and Sarah Duncan.

14

Heat at the Meet

Early the following morning, Mikayla was preparing for her second day at the track. She was mildly surprised at how calm she was, given the disastrous and rather bizarre experiences of the day before. Her thoughts were on her mother, but not in any kind of mournful way. She was remembering her mother's determination to communicate with her in the hospital. The strength and power of those few words Noelle had been able to utter were with her still.

Mikayla phoned David when she was ready to leave and arranged to meet him at their usual corner. As she was packing a lunch into her bag, her foster mother appeared at the kitchen door. "Are you sure you want to go to the meet today, Mik?" Jan asked with concern. "I'm certain Ms. Bradford would understand, given the circumstances."

"You're right, Jan, she would," Mikayla replied. "But I need to do this and I really believe this is what my mother would want me to do." Jan regarded Mikayla for a long moment, then approached her and, slowly, as if she thought Mikayla might reject the gesture, put her arms around her foster daughter. Mikayla, unaccustomed to displays of physical affection from her reserved foster mother, did not respond immediately. When she did return the hug, it brought them both closer to tears than they wished to be.

Breaking the embrace, Mikayla picked up her bag and moved to the door. "Thanks, Jan, for … um, for making my lunch. I forgot to do that last night."

"You're welcome, Mikayla, I didn't mind at all," Jan replied awkwardly. "Good luck today!"

Mikayla gave a little wave as she went out the door.

* * *

When Mikayla and David arrived in the schoolyard, they joined their friends who were talking about their parents' last minute warnings to stay out of the sun as much as possible.

"Hey, Mik, this must be a record, you being at school before me two days in a row!" Victoria laughed as she joined the group a few minutes later.

Mikayla smiled.

"Let's hope it's not the only record we set today," David piped in.

The happy, busy chatter continued as the small group boarded the bus for Terry Fox. They speculated on how hot it would get as the day progressed, for they were already sweating and it wasn't yet seven o'clock.

* * *

Max was the first one to fall prey to the unusually blistering spring sun. Running hard to keep up with a Hopevale runner in the 3000-metre race, Max collapsed at the finish line, dehydrated and suffering from heat exhaustion, but not before he took the race in the final twenty metres to capture the gold medal. Max was taken to the air-conditioned first aid trailer and was feeling better after some water and a rest.

The meet conveners discussed whether the remainder of the meet should be cancelled because of the extreme heat, but it was decided that, with the most demanding event now completed, coaches would be advised to warn their students to stay out of the sun when not competing and drink lots of water.

After making sure that Max would indeed survive, Mikayla and Victoria headed across the infield to the shot put circle where several of the pentathletes had gathered to start warming up.

"Warm up. Ha! What a laugh," remarked Mikayla. "If we were any warmer, we'd melt."

"Actually," Victoria answered, "my dad says that track athletes do better in this kind of weather because the muscles and joints *are* so warm."

"Well, I guess we'll find out, won't we?" quipped Mikayla. "If I manage to make any decent throws, it's gotta be the heat!"

Hearing herself make a joke, Mikayla reflected guiltily on her gravely ill mother. She knew that allowing herself to dwell on the situation would cause her spirits to plummet. On the other hand, she could not help but believe that her mother had practically given her a mission the evening before: to be strong and to pursue her dreams. Mikayla did not know how she would do today, but she had already vowed to dedicate her very best effort to her mother.

All the pentathletes had by now arrived in the competition area. While they were warming up, Mikayla took the opportunity to assess each girl's body type to see if she could pick out the most likely shot-putters. All but two of the top competitors were built similarly to Mikayla, tall and lean. Mikayla thought herself to be one of the more muscular athletes, but she knew from the experience of many practices that she didn't seem to have the necessary weight to hurl the three kilogram shot any significant distance. Her best throw ever had been 8.05 metres, which was really quite mediocre.

The official gave instructions and announced the order of the competitors. Mikayla had dropped to fifth place overall following her fifth-place finish in the long jump. The seven points separating her from the leader would, she knew, be almost impossible to make up, but that was no longer what was driving her.

During the first round, Mikayla followed her pattern of not watching the other competitors. Her own throw was good for her, eight metres exactly. But it was only the sixth-best throw of the round.

The second round was underway when Victoria nudged Mikayla lightly. "Check out Bonnie's style, Mik. She looks so professional!"

Mikayla watched as the competitor from Hopevale, currently holding down third place overall, tucked the heavy metal sphere under her ear, then hopped backwards from a low crouch, pivoting toward the target area and releasing the shot forcefully. It arced through the air and landed in the sand almost at the ten-metre marker.

"Wow! That's not how Mr. Daniels taught us to do it!" exclaimed Mikayla. "Watch me, Tori. Is this what she did?"

Victoria observed as Mikayla tried to duplicate the throwing style of the athlete who had just competed.

"Try and get a little lower, Mik. Yeah, that's it," Victoria coached her friend. "Now, hop, hop, step and pivot. Good! Okay, now try it again. It's almost your turn."

Mikayla's name was called. She ignored the shot laying on the ground in the circle and assumed her new starting position. She tried the unfamiliar approach twice before picking up the shot and resting it in the notch of her neck below her ear. Taking a deep breath and trying to visualize her own movements, Mikayla burst from the crouch, spinning and releasing the shot with an accompanying shout. The heavy metal sphere flew through the air, landing just beyond the nine-metre mark.

Mikayla could hardly believe her eyes. She looked to where Victoria was standing with her mouth hanging open and both listened excitedly as the official called out the measurement of 9.10 metres. At that, Mikayla bounded over to her friend and they grabbed each others' hands, jumping up and down and laughing delightedly.

Mikayla's final throw was just short of nine metres, but her second-round effort was good enough to give her a completely unexpected third place in the event. Mikayla had now moved into a tie for fourth place in the pentathlon. The other competitor who shared fourth place with her was Jessie Tremaine, Amelie's old friend from Queen Victoria Middle School. With a first in shot put, Hopevale's Bonnie Tam became the overall event leader with 42 points, six points ahead of Mikayla and Jessie. In between were girls from Broadbent Junior High and Emily Carr Middle School. The championship would be decided in the final event. The 800-metre run would take place in mid-afternoon, at the height of the day's heat.

At the lunch break Ms. Bradford and Mr. Daniels offered to supervise the team at Mooney's Bay so they could cool off. The popular beach, located on the Rideau River, was especially busy because of the unusually hot weather. Parents with young children, people playing volleyball, and senior citizens enjoying a picnic had all converged with students and coaches from the track to try and seek relief from the intense heat. The half-hour or so spent playing in the water refreshed the McClung athletes. Even the coaches went in and joined their students, throwing frisbees and splashing around like children. Afterwards, the team enjoyed their lunch in the shaded picnic area near the water.

15

The Big Race

The time of the final pentathlon event was approaching. Mikayla excused herself from the company of her friends and made her way across the end of the track to where a picnic table sat under a small cluster of trees. She perched on the end of the wooden table and rummaged through her sports bag for her running shoes. As she was lacing them up, she remembered Amelie's letter and sifted again through the cluttered bag, finding the wrinkled blue sheets at the bottom.

Mikayla could almost hear Amelie's voice as she read her message again. She re-familiarized herself with the advice about racing against Amelie's former friend and she closed her eyes and pondered Amelie's encouragement to believe in herself.

Her mother's words from the night before came back to her too. She had said to be strong and to make her own dreams come true. Something she was never able to do for herself, Mikayla thought sadly. Well, she continued in thought, I can't change that for her now, but I *can* try to believe in myself.

With that thought in mind, Mikayla headed toward the 800-metre starting line, in response to the announcer's first call. As the sun blazed overhead, the other pentathletes stretched lethargically on the grass. A few gave a little wave or smiled a greeting to Mikayla as she approached.

"Hi, Mikayla," Jessie Tremaine said, patting the grass next to her to indicate that she wanted Mikayla to sit down. "So we're tied, eh? I heard you never beat Ammi in the 800. That surprises me; I didn't think she was very strong at that distance."

Mikayla looked at Jessie for a moment before answering. "Ammi is an awesome 800-metre runner. Maybe the training and competition she had before she came to McClung didn't bring out the best in her."

Jessie stared, open-mouthed, at Mikayla. She had obviously not expected such an unfriendly response.

Mikayla used the pause to move over next to Bonnie Tam.

"Hey, Bonnie, are you ever flexible!" Mikayla remarked. Bonnie was folded over her legs with her head resting comfortably on her knees.

"That's from tae kwon do," Bonnie replied, without changing her position. "We have to do a lot of flexibility exercises to be able to kick high and not injure ourselves."

"Tae kwon do? Cool," said Mikayla. "What belt do you have?"

"I'm testing for blue next month. I don't know if I'll get it; there's a ton of stuff to remember. Plus, I've got to break through five boards for it. I'm still working on that."

"Wow! No wonder you're in such good shape!" Mikayla observed admiringly.

Just then the clerk of the course began his instructions to the pentathletes. The 800 was the only event in which the athletes would all participate together.

When they were led out onto the track, the girls were lined up in their order from the inside lane along a curved starting line. Mikayla stood on the track with four runners, including Jessie, on her left, and the other seven on her right.

The race would be two full laps of the track, taking somewhere between two and a half and three minutes to run.

Mikayla thought that at least two of the girls looked as if they should not compete. They already appeared overheated, red-faced and unfocused.

The starter was in place and ready with his gun. Mikayla glanced at Jessie who avoided looking back at her. Her face had a determined set and Mikayla realized that she had probably succeeded in making Jessie angry enough to run the race of her life.

Taking her usual standing position as the starter began his commands, Mikayla let go of all thought except the race before her. When the gun sounded, the field of competitors took off quickly. Mikayla was immediately aware of all the runners converging from the right, jockeying for position on the inside, leaving her toward the back of the middle pack of runners.

Half a head taller than the others, Mikayla could easily see ahead to where Jessie Tremaine was moving swiftly up toward the front of the still closely-packed runners. Fortunately, Mikayla was not boxed in and was able to pull out and pass three competitors, moving up next to Bonnie who was directly behind Jessie. Mikayla knew she could not keep running in the second lane; it would mean too much extra distance. Just then, a space opened up between Bonnie and Jessie. Mikayla slipped into lane one.

Amelie had been right. Jessie liked to go out fast and, for one awful moment, Mikayla recalled the first time she'd run the 800 in Heritage Park. She just hoped her own stamina had improved enough that this race would not end as that one had.

Mikayla was aware of Bonnie still close behind. She glanced back quickly and saw that the runners were now strung out in a long line behind them and they hadn't even completed a lap yet. Jessie was running a very strong race and Mikayla could already see, as she rounded the final turn of the first lap, that three of the pentathletes had succumbed to the heat and had slowed almost to a walk around the 200-metre mark. If everyone stayed in the race, several girls would actually be lapped by the leaders the second time around. Another quick glance around told Mikayla that Bonnie had dropped back several strides and that the next group of four runners was well behind her, followed by the stragglers. Two girls, the ones Mikayla had identified earlier as overheated, were now walking.

As they entered the second curve of the second and final lap, Mikayla felt Jessie making a move to establish a bigger lead. The pace was very fast, but Mikayla felt strong and comfortable. She decided to give Jessie her lead for the next 100 metres, then try and go by her over the last 200.

With Mikayla's eyes fixed on her back, Jessie started to weave on the track, just a little bit at first, then more noticeably, her feet no longer planting in a straight, steady path. Mikayla increased her speed to close the gap between herself and the faltering girl. Suddenly, with just over 100 metres remaining in the race, Jessie crumpled onto the track. Because of her speed, Mikayla had to leap over Jessie to avoid stepping on her. Immediately, she halted her own progress and turned back to the fallen girl.

Jessie was conscious but seemed to be in very bad shape and bleeding from the scrapes she had gotten in the fall. Mikayla lifted Jessie's head and rested it in her lap.

"Help's on the way, Jess. You'll be fine," Mikayla assured the injured girl. Bonnie had caught up and was kneeling next to Mikayla, holding Jessie's hand.

"You two girls finish the race." It was the clerk of the course who had arrived with Jessie's coach and the physiotherapist carrying a water bottle and first aid kit.

The only other girls still running in the event were approaching the scene but did not appear to pose any competitive threat; they were simply trying to complete the run on their feet. Three girls had dropped out altogether.

Bonnie and Mikayla resumed their positions in the first lane of the track and, when Mikayla looked back over her shoulder at Bonnie before starting to run, an unspoken understanding passed between them. There would be no race.

They began to jog the last 100 metres toward the finish line, Mikayla in front, Bonnie, a stride's distance behind her. The two girls crossed the finish line to an explosion of cheering and clapping from the bleachers.

From under their enormous sun umbrella, Victoria, David and Max shouted as loud as their already hoarse voices would allow, starting a McClung chorus of "MIK! MIK! MIK!" while neighbouring Hopevale students screamed "BON-NIE! BON-NIE!" Soon, the two schools were cooperating in chant, alternating the names of the two girls, now heroes to both schools.

As Mikayla and Bonnie rejoiced over having successfully completed the gruelling run, track officials prepared to announce the results of the pentathlon competition.

* * *

The final awards ceremony was just getting underway. McClung maintained its success rate by capturing the meet championship for the tenth year in a row.

At the podium, the pentathlon medal ceremony was about to begin. As Mikayla looked into the crowd of student and parent supporters, she heard her name announced. She hopped up onto the second-place step, lowering her head so that the meet director could hang the silver medallion around her neck. Her performances in the shot put and the 800-metre run had moved her into a better position than she had dreamed possible after the disastrous results of the previous day. More importantly, she had fulfilled her mother's request that she be strong and make her own dreams come true.

She heard the chant of "MIK!" repeated again from the stands and smiled broadly, waving at her friends. She saw Victoria with her parents and sister. David's mom and dad were there, too, one snapping photographs while the other pointed the video camera toward the podium.

As Bonnie Tam, the gold medalist, received her award to loud cheering from the stands, Mikayla saw that Jan and Taylor were at the fence. Behind them, she saw Jason and Ms. Duncan. She watched as Jason bent down and hoisted Angeline up onto his shoulders. Mikayla felt her eyes fill up. Another dream had come true. Her family had come to the meet!

But as she was rejoicing over her family's attendance, it occurred to her that Ms. Duncan's presence at the track was unexpected. And then, suddenly, without understanding how, she knew. It was her mother. She must have ...

The tears spilled over, and Mikayla felt the slowing of the roller coaster she'd been riding for the last two days. She stepped off the podium and walked slowly toward the fence where her family awaited her.

Epilogue

The Victory

Mikayla couldn't believe that a whole year had passed, and she had to shake her head to clear away the memories. Today, she was already the pentathlon champion, whether she made this jump or not. But breaking the record symbolized for her the last hurdle in the quest, begun a year ago, to overcome her self-doubt and achieve her dreams.

The officials were ready. Her friends were watching from the bleachers. She looked over at David, Victoria and Pauline and smiled reassuringly at them. Her family was there too: Jan and Taylor, Jason and Angeline. Even the Lincolns, who had adopted Angeline and had recently moved into the city, were there, watching with expectant smiles. Mikayla was overjoyed, but now the time had come to concentrate on the task before her.

Glancing over at her coach one last time, Mikayla gave a little nod before focusing on the crossbar. After a moment, she started her approach to the potentially record-breaking jump. Each step was light, but deliberate, as she closed in on her objective.

She lifted off, felt herself soar through the air, her back arching. She finished with a powerful snap of her legs to clear her feet and then felt the give of the crash pad as she landed. Laying still, Mikayla held her breath for the instant it took her to realize that the bar was still in place. Suddenly the screams of her friends and teammates broke the silence. She hurled herself off the mat and flew to her coach.

"Ms. Bradford," Mikayla cried, "how can I ever thank you?"

"For what?" the coach smiled, her hands on Mikayla's shoulders as she regarded her while seeming to compose her response. "It was *you* who made that spectacular jump and broke an ancient record. It was *your* strength and courage that brought you through the past year and created today's success, *and* your victory." Then she hugged her, and Mikayla felt her coach's tears on her cheek.

Moments later, as Mikayla bowed her head to receive the pentathlon gold medal, she flashed back once again to the previous year. So many things had happened since her mother's death. It had been hard, the hardest thing she'd ever gone through, but she had found the strength she needed to get herself and Angeline through it and to look to her own future. Considering these thoughts, she recalled Coach Bradford's words from moments earlier and at last understood. Her victory — her real victory — was about something far greater than all the gold medals and broken records in the world.

Other books you'll enjoy in the Sports Stories series...

Baseball

☐ *Curve Ball* by John Danakas #1
Tom Poulos is looking forward to a summer of baseball in Toronto until his mother puts him on a plane to Winnipeg.

☐ *Baseball Crazy* by Martyn Godfrey #10
Rob Carter wins an all-expenses-paid chance to be batboy at the Blue Jays' spring training camp in Florida.

☐ *Shark Attack* by Judi Peers #25
The East City Sharks have a good chance of winning the county championship until their arch rivals get a tough new pitcher.

Basketball

☐ *Fast Break* by Michael Coldwell #8
Moving from Toronto to small-town Nova Scotia was rough, but when Jeff makes the school basketball team he thinks things are looking up.

☐ *Camp All-Star* by Michael Coldwell #12
In this insider's view of a basketball camp, Jeff Lang encounters some unexpected challenges.

☐ *Nothing but Net* by Michael Coldwell #18
The Cape Breton Grizzly Bears face an out-of-town basketball tournament they're sure to lose.

☐ *Slam Dunk* by Steven Barwin and Gabriel David Tick #23
In this sequel to *Roller Hockey Blues*, Mason Ashbury's basketball team adjusts to the arrival of some new players: girls.

Figure Skating

☐ *A Stroke of Luck* by Kathryn Ellis #6
Strange accidents are stalking one of the skaters at the Millwood Arena.

☐ *The Winning Edge* by Michele Martin Bosley #28
Jennie wants more than anything to win a grueling series of competitions, but is success worth losing her friends?

Gymnastics

☐ *The Perfect Gymnast* by Michele Martin Bossley #9
Abby's new friend has all the confidence she needs, but she also has a serious problem that nobody but Abby seems to know about.

Ice hockey

☐ *Shoot to Score* by Sandra Richmond #31
Playing defence on the B list, alongside the coach's mean-spirited son, are tough obstacles for Steven to overcome, but he perseveres and changes his luck.

☐ *Two Minutes for Roughing* by Joseph Romain #2
As a new player on a tough Toronto hockey team, Les must fight to fit in.

☐ *Hockey Night in Transcona* by John Danakas #7
Cody Powell gets promoted to the Transcona Sharks' first line, bumping out the coach's son who's not happy with the change.

☐ *Face Off* by C.A. Forsyth #13
A talented hockey player finds himself competing with his best friend for a spot on a select team.

☐ *Hat Trick* by Jacqueline Guest #20
The only girl on an all-boys' hockey team works to earn the captain's respect and her mother's approval.

☐ *Hockey Heroes* by John Danakas #22
A left-winger on the thirteen-year-old Transcona Sharks adjusts to a new best friend and his mom's boyfriend.

☐ *Hockey Heat Wave* by C.A. Forsyth #27
In this sequel to *Face Off*, Zack and Mitch encounter some trouble when it looks like only one of them will make the select team at hockey camp.

Riding

☐ *A Way With Horses* by Peter McPhee #11
A young Alberta rider invited to study show jumping at a posh local riding school uncovers a secret.

☐ *Riding Scared* by Marion Crook #15
A reluctant new rider struggles to overcome her fear of horses.

☐ *Katie's Midnight Ride* by C.A. Forsyth #16
An ambitious barrel racer finds herself without a horse weeks before her biggest rodeo.

☐ *Glory Ride* by Tamara L. Williams #21
Chloe Anderson fights memories of a tragic fall for a place on the Ontario Young Riders' Team.

☐ *Cutting it Close* by Marion Crook #24
In this novel about barrel racing, a talented young rider finds her horse is in trouble just as she is about to compete in an important event.

Roller hockey

☐ *Roller Hockey Blues* by Steven Barwin and Gabriel David Tick #17
Mason Ashbury faces a summer of boredom until he makes the roller-hockey team.

Running

☐ *Fast Finish* by Bill Swan #30
Noah is a promising young runner headed for the provincial finals when he suddenly decides to withdraw from the event.

Sailing

☐ *Sink or Swim* by William Pasnak #5
Dario can barely manage the dog paddle, but thanks to his mother he's spending the summer at a water sports camp.

Soccer

☐ *Lizzie's Soccer Showdown* by John Danakas #3
When Lizzie asks why the boys and girls can't play together, she finds herself the new captain of the soccer team.

Swimming

☐ *Breathing Not Required* by Michele Martin Bossley #4
An eager synchronized swimmer works hard to be chosen for a solo and almost loses her best friend in the process.

☐ *Water Fight!* by Michele Martin Bossley #14
Josie's perfect sister is driving her crazy but when she takes up swimming — Josie's sport — it's too much to take.

☐ *Taking a Dive* by Michele Martin Bossley #19
Josie holds the provincial record for the butterfly, but in this sequel to *Water Fight,* she can't seem to match her own time and might not go on to the nationals.

☐ *Great Lengths* by Sandra Diersch #26
Fourteen-year-old Jessie decides to find out whether the rumours about a new swimmer at her Vancouver club are true.

Track and Field

☐ *Mikayla's Victory* by Cynthia Bates #29
Mikayla must compete against her friend if she wants to represent her school at an important track event.